M000307934

GEORGE AND THE ANGELS

Look for these other great Beachfront titles:

By Glenn Meganck—

It's A Young, Young World

For Children—

Big Deal
Big Deal At The Center Of The Earth
No Big Deal

By J.R. Ripley—

Tony Kozol mysteries:

Stiff In The Freezer
Skulls Of Sedona
Lost In Austin
The Body From Ipanema
Bum Rap In Branson

Gendarme Charles Trenet novels:

Murder In St. Barts
Death Of A Cheat

By Marie Celine—

Dishing Up Death

By Nick Lucas—

Five Minutes

—Beachfront Publishing—
"Independent Publishing for Independent Minds."

GEORGE AND THE ANGELS

Glenn Meganck

Beachfront Publishing

This is a work of fiction. Any resemblances to actual places or events, or persons, living or dead, is purely coincidental.

Copyright © 2006 Glenn Meganck

All rights reserved under international and Pan-American Copyright Conventions. Published in the United States by Beachfront Publishing.

No part of this book may be used or reproduced in any manner without the written consent of the publisher, with the exception of brief passages contained in critical articles or reviews.

Beachfront Publishing, POB 811922, Boca Raton, FL 33481. Correspond with Beachfront via email at:
    Info@BeachfrontEntertainment.com

First edition March 2006

Library of Congress Cataloging-in-Publication Data

Meganck, Glenn, date
    George and the Angels / Glenn Meganck
    p. cm.
    ISBN: 978-1-892339-59-1 / 1-892339-59-5
       1. Psychiatric hospital patients – Fiction. 2. Auditory hallucinations – Fiction. 3. Angels – Fiction. I. Title.

PS3613.E38 G46 2006
813'.54 – dc22   2005053095

Printed in the United States of America

I really, honestly, do not believe in time. Except as a conceptual crutch that helps us hobble through this world. And there's nothing wrong with that. However, I believe that everything exists at all times. Really, I do. I don't believe in evolution either. And I'm not speaking about creationism vs. evolution, so let's not go there. I'm speaking about change for the better. Things change, sure. For the better? That's pretty subjective.

I do believe that reality is what each and every one of us create for ourselves. No two are alike. Like snowflakes, if you believe that. And we form it, mend it and amend it a bit each day; some days more dramatically than others.

Of course, when five billion realities pressed together on one chunk of rock collide, things can get rather chaotic. How could they not? Nonetheless, we're all pretty much alike, though some of us may be labeled more crazy, cruel, lazy or indifferent, than the norm. That's okay, too.

What follows on these pages is exactly what happened as best as I can remember. That's important. I did not create the story, I remembered it. This is important to the story, so I hope you will remember this, whether you believe the tale or not.

So. Crazy, cruel, lazy, indifferent? Fiction, fantasy, autobiography? Okay, so I should add insane rambling. There, does that make some of you happy? Labels are great for pasting to cans of green beans. Beyond that, they seem rather dubious to me.

But then, at this point in time, I could be labeled crazy—

G

—1—

"I am not crazy I am not crazy I am not crazy I am not—"

"Mr. Richards?"

"—crazy I am not crazy I am not crazy I am not crazy I am not crazy I—"

The attendant cleared her throat. Her hand clutched the door handle tentatively as a skittish dragonfly. Mr. Richards' back was to her and he was facing the open window. Sunlight bathed his front side while his back was as dark as the dark side of the moon.

She could tell he was speaking, but it was a low drone and the words indistinguishable. "Mr. Richards . . ."

"—am not crazy I am not crazy I am not crazy I am—"

She spoke more loudly this time. "George."

Mr. Richards turned, his mouth half open. He looked at her for a moment, as though lost, and then spoke. "Yes?"

The attendant tilted her head toward the open hallway. "It's time to go."

"Go?"

"Yes, it's time to go, George."

George took a last look out the window. Biscayne Bay, pounded by the southern light, dazzled the eyes like the liquid shimmering of a blue-skinned alien. Or was he the alien?

He turned to go. "Are you sure, Mary?" With a pale hand and a weak grip, George picked up the beaten little suitcase he'd brought with him to the sanitarium. He had sympathy for the little suitcase. They had both been beaten by forces never seen.

Mary nodded. "Yes, George."

He obediently followed the officious attendant along the echoing corridors of the Miami Institute of Health. A polite name for a place that kept loonies under lock and key. The suitcase slapped against his right leg as Mary turned a corner, passed a nurses' station and held open a door that normally stood bolted—keeping damaged people like George from the real people on the other side.

George stopped several paces behind, set down his little suitcase, adjusted his thin brown tie, took a little breath, remembering what Dr. Grossman had said about breathing exercises—slow and easy, George. . .slow and easy. . .I am not crazy I am not crazy. . .

He looked at his feet. Were his dull brown shoes speaking to him? I am not crazy I am not crazy. . .

"George?"

George looked up. There was Elaine, his wife. Looking like she always did.

In twenty-three years of marriage, she'd barely aged at all. She'd been pretty when he'd met her and she was pretty still. Her eyes were the color of raked autumn leaves. Brown hair fell naturally past her shoulders. Her face was soft and well-chiseled, with barely a wrinkle, except when she was concerned or worried. Like she appeared now and the space between her eyebrows dug itself a furrow that a finger could trace even in the dark.

George jiggled his suitcase and stopped in the open doorway. "Thank you, Mary."

"You take care of yourself, George." She gave him a friendly pat on the arm, straightening the edges of his coat. "Have some fun now."

George smiled weakly. "Fun. Yes. Goodbye."

"Goodbye, George. Goodbye, Mrs. Richards."

Mrs. Richards said goodbye to the aide, then hugged her husband. He opened his arms wide, suspending the suitcase in the air. "It's good to see you, darling. You look well."

George knew Elaine was only saying this. He looked well? Was that supposed to make him well? Inside? In his head, where it mattered the most? "Thanks."

"Tim is outside with the car."

"Tim? You brought Tim here?"

"Yes, he wanted to see you."

George was shaking his head. "I wish you hadn't done that, Elaine. I don't want him to see me. . ." he paused, then said, "like this. You know that."

"He's your son, and he's missed you. It's been over a month. I couldn't tell him no, could I? And I didn't bring him inside. Besides, he thinks you were ill. That's all anyone's told him—"

"I have been ill," George said, his tone scoffing.

"You know what I mean, George. We told Tim and Claire that you were sick, contagious."

George, shoulders bent, head down, started for the door. "Don't worry, one thing I am not is contagious."

Elaine sighed and ran to keep up. This was not the reunion she'd rehearsed over and over in her head. Why couldn't life stick to the plan once in a while?

George let Tim do the driving. After all, the kid had turned sixteen and was now the proud possessor of a driver's license. Besides, George felt guilty. He'd missed Tim's sixteenth birthday two weeks ago because he'd been in treatment. Doc Grossman had even forbidden him to call his son to wish him a happy birthday. Grossman said it might be too depressing for both Tim and George. So, not a word. Mum's the word.

How depressing was that?

It was going to be a good, solid hour of driving from Miami to Boca Raton. I-95 ran from one town to the other like a jagged, clogged and narrow artery with tens of thousands of deadly, four-wheeled blood cells running rampant, running blind. George was just as glad not to be doing the driving.

He shut his eyes and tilted his head back until it touched the headrest, stretched out his legs in the roomy backseat, while his son wrestled with the wheel of the Mercedes. It was the big one. The flagship of Mercedes Benz; polished Almandine black exterior with java Nappa leather interior and burl walnut trim. It was the best, of course, with more bells and whistles than he could keep track of or even remember how to use without checking the thick, Byzantine owner's manual.

The Richards always had the best. The best that their money could buy, in any case. And why shouldn't they? as Elaine was always saying. They were quite well-to-do and all the neighbors drove expensive, elitist automobiles. Why shouldn't they? And how would it look if they didn't?

George now and again threatened to buy a Honda Accord or maybe a Toyota Camry. How about a four door Hyundai? That always got Elaine churned up. The only folks with cars of that caliber in their neighborhood were the domestic workers. Porsche, Mercedes, Lexus and BMWs were all common as tap water in Boca Raton, Florida. George sometimes wondered how his kids would handle the real world when the time came.

And it would, of course.

His wife sat beside him, droning on and on, like a one-person reenactment of the events of the month he'd been away. It didn't sound like he'd missed much—his wife's aunt had some minor health troubles, stuff about the kids' school, some day to day office difficulties that he wouldn't have cared about on the best of days—a whole lot of nothing.

Nothing.

The tires droned on over the pavement. Over a whole lot of Nothing.

Spinning.

Spinning over a whole lot of nothing. Spinning spinning spinning. Nowhere nowhere nowhere. *I am not crazy I am not—*

He closed his eyes more tightly, trying to drown out the sound of her voice and the agony of his son's tentative driving.

"I'm just so glad you'll be home for Thanksgiving," Elaine was saying.

"Gobble, gobble," said George.

"What?"

"I'm practicing. I was thinking maybe I'd get a big turkey suit and dress up for Thanksgiving. Hey, I could come down the chimney," he said, "with a sack full of stuffing!"

Tim snorted. "Funny, Dad."

Elaine shook her head. "You keep your eyes on the road, please," she exhorted.

Tim released a half-scowl. He figured Mom should lighten up on his dad. So what if the guy had a few problems? Didn't everybody? He was still a great guy and a great dad. Tim tightened his grip on the wheel. It was cool to drive, especially such a great machine. When he was old enough, he was going to get a cool car, too. Maybe a Mercedes SL or a

911 Carrera.

"Everybody's coming," Elaine said to her husband.

"Really," replied George. His eyes were still closed. "How exciting for everybody."

"You know what I mean. I've invited your mother, both your sisters . . ."

His wife's cloying voice faded into the distance as George's mind drifted in other directions. How lucky Elaine was that her mother and father were gone and her siblings far away. He'd never gotten on with his family. Talk about aliens. He wouldn't be surprised if some biologist took skin samples of the bunch of them and discovered that George was of a different species altogether from his Richards' kin.

He opened his eyes. "You know I don't get along with them."

Elaine set a hand on his thigh. "But it's the holidays. You have to try."

George looked at her blankly. "Why?" Inwardly he smiled. That had stopped her. After all, why the hell did he have to try? Because it was the holidays? So the hell what? He'd been trying to one degree or another for forty long years. Wasn't that enough?

"George."

According to George, Elaine had a sixteen page dictionary full of Georges, sixteen Georges to a page; and each and every George was said with a different inflection and possessed a unique definition all its own, only the spelling remained consistently the same. This was George Number

73, page 5, line 9. Definition: *Oh, come on now. That's no way to behave. I'm making an effort. Why can't you?*

George shut his eyes and nodded. "Can we stop somewhere?"

"What did you have in mind?"

"The ocean? How about the Pompano Fishing Pier?" George didn't fish. Didn't even like the idea. But he loved to walk out on the boards and smell the sea, watch the egrets, seagulls, and pelicans, feel himself bathed by the cool breeze that swept across from Africa somewhere.

"Sure, Dad."

"I'm afraid there's no time for that." Elaine tapped her platinum Piaget watch. "I have to get back to the office. Two of the girls are out. I thought you'd want to go also. But maybe you'd like Tim to drop you off at the house instead?"

"No," answered George with a voice as flat-lined as his spirit. "The office. The office will be fine."

The office, headquarters of Richards Medical Transcription Services, Incorporated, was fifteen hundred square feet of space which, from George's point of view, was an annex of Hell itself. Leased, of course. There were three, gray stuccoed, gray roofed, one story buildings in the small office park, forming a U around a long, central fountain. RMTS occupied approximately half of building three, at the bottom of the U.

Tim parked the car in the space reserved for Elaine and George put on his happy face.

"You'd better pick up Claire from school," Mrs. Richards told her son. "Then you go straight home."

"Yes, Mom."

"Pick us up at five. No, wait." She kissed Tim on the cheek. "Make that five-fifteen. We'll all go out to dinner, so dress and make sure Claire does, too."

"Okay, Mom." Tim jumped behind the wheel and closed the car door before she could say anymore.

Elaine took her husband's arm. "I thought we'd go to that new Chinese place. Won't that be fun?"

George nodded. He held open the office door, then paused, realizing he'd already lost his happy face. He looked at the ground—the sidewalk was gray—swallowed, slapped on his happy face, and entered his own little piece of Hell. Leased, of course, triple net.

The flat, office carpet was gray as an elephant's hide. The desks were gray and two of the employees had gray hair. As George and Elaine walked in, heads looked up from their computer screens—the computers were gray—and welcomed George back.

George forced himself to be sociable for a minute or two and then the faces returned to their computer screens and headphones went back in the ladies' ears and feet went back to the ladies' pedals. The life of a medical transcriptionist was one long TypeFest. And George hated it. He always had. The only thing good about it was the money.

Without RTMS, what would he be? Answer: Forty-six years old, balding, paunchy and poor. George Richards the

Loser. Now, he was George Richards the Winner, president of Richards Medical Transcription Services.

Lucky him.

George grabbed a bottle of soda water from the refrigerator in the break area and retreated behind the gray panels of his cubicle. This was his hidey-place and he'd had it built especially for himself. All the employees worked out in the main room, connected to computers and phone lines over which the doctors from the various hospitals dictated their reports. Elaine's desk, while in the same room as George's, was exposed, facing a window which looked out over the employees. She liked to keep an eye on things, she did.

George had ordered the cubicle walls for himself, effectively blocking out himself from the world and the world from him. The portable walls had only been available in gray, the color of ashes, from a fire that had long ago gone cold. Gray wasn't George's favorite color, but he'd grown used to it.

George liked to hide. He didn't want anyone to know he was there. He didn't want anybody to see him. He didn't want anyone, not even strangers, knowing what he did for a living. He was president of Richards Medical Transcription Services, but everybody, including the employees, thought Elaine was. And, of course, this was just the way George liked it.

He put his hands on his desk. There was a light coating of dust over his keyboard and papers. No one was allowed to touch his desk, not even to clean it. He didn't like anything moved. A month's worth of nothingness had accumulated.

He yawned, suddenly feeling terribly sleepy, almost drugged. But that was nothing. That was normal.

"Are you alright back there, honey?"

"Yes, I'm fine." He pushed his hands into his face, struggling to stay awake. He turned on the computer and pretended to work.

He hated work. He hated medical transcription. He hated sticking those little foam thingies in his ears and stepping on that stupid pedal until his foot hurt, listening to the voices that came spilling out incessantly in his ears; voices speaking of other peoples' miseries and ailments. It was all so depressing.

And his hands hurt and his wrists hurt and his head hurt. And he felt like a goddamn monkey. And he hated being nothing but a trained goddamn monkey.

They were all trained goddamn monkeys.

In private, he always called the employees of Richards Medical Transcription Services, Inc. Elaine's pets. She hated that. But that's what they were. They were all her pets. Her trained goddamn monkeys.

—2—

Tim arrived right on schedule.

He was a good son. Claire was with him and she burst through the office door, all energy and smiles. She said hi to her mom and leapt into her father's arms, practically bringing down the temporary gray walls.

"Hiya, Blue Eyes," George said. He kissed his daughter's smooth forehead and she kissed him back.

"I missed you, Daddy." She proudly held up a sheet of white paper, upon which she'd drawn a wobbly looking man holding hands with a little girl. She'd written their names, Daddy and Claire, beneath in jagged Crayon.

"That's beautiful, Claire." George gave his daughter another hug. "I missed you, too. This much." He held his arms outstretched. His fingers touched the walls.

Claire mimicked him. "Well, I missed you this much," she said, nearly matching his stretch. She was big for an eight year old.

George rummaged through his desk until he found a pushpin. "I'll just stick this picture right here." And he tacked the picture to the wall with a grin.

"Ready, George?"

"Yes, Elaine." He took his daughter's hand. Her warm little hand felt good in his. He hadn't realized until that moment just how much he'd missed holding hands with his little girl.

"Can I drive, Dad?" begged Tim.

"No, let's let your father drive. I'm sure he'd rather," answered Elaine, fielding the question for her husband.

George shrugged for his son's benefit, as if to say 'whatever.'

George followed Elaine's directions to the Chinese restaurant as she shared all the glowing reviews she'd been hearing from all her friends about the place. It was up near Mizner Park, a trendy shopping and dining development on Federal Highway. China Garden was the new, 'in' place to go and so they went.

The young waiter led them to a table in the middle but George insisted on the empty booth in the corner and he took the seat facing the wall, so he wouldn't have to see anyone but his family. Claire squeezed in beside him. "How's school?"

"Okay," replied Claire, fiddling with her napkin and silverware.

"How about you, Tim?"

"Okay, I guess."

Tim and Claire, though eight years apart, attended the same private school in Boca—a school that charged through the nose for tuition and yet still managed, on a near weekly basis, to hit the parents up for additional contributions, for books, buildings, computers, et ceteras. Et ceteras didn't come cheap. Their needs were endless. Money money money. Schools needed money. They all needed money.

George nodded. Everything was okay, he guessed. China Garden was crowded and noisy. It seemed like everyone had something to say but him. Paper lanterns hung from the ceiling. Dragons stalked the walls. George ordered the steamed vegetables, brown rice and bean curd.

"I'm thinking of buying a boat," George announced midway through his meal. He had no appetite and the food had no taste, but the others seemed to be enjoying their selections.

"What? Elaine dropped her spring roll.

"A boat, you know."

"Cool, Dad."

"I want a boat! I want a boat!" cried Claire.

"A boat, George? Whatever for? You don't even know anything about boats or boating. You can't be serious." She dipped her spring roll in orange sauce and bit off the end.

"But I am serious," insisted George. "And I could take one of those Coast Guard courses. I've seen them advertised in the papers."

"But George—" Elaine looked less than amused. "Where

would you even keep it?"

"I don't know. We could move to the Intracoastal. Get a house on the water?"

"Yeah!" hollered Tim. "What kind of boat are we getting, Dad? A sailboat? A motor boat? A yacht?"

"Can we sleep on it?" wondered Claire.

George laughed. "I don't know. At least not yet. I mean, we'll have to look around, see what there is. Do some boat shopping."

The kids were nodding enthusiastically.

"We cannot move to the Intracoastal, George," said Elaine, refusing to be caught up in the fantasy of owning a boat. "We already have a house and we love it."

George didn't want to fight in front of the kids, so he didn't say that the only person who loved the house was Elaine. After all, she'd spent eighteen months in her spare time working with some hotshot Boca architect building the thing. And yes, it was nice, but no, he didn't love it. He'd have been happy with a little house on the water. The kind he used to dream of owning even as a kid.

Sure, the place they had now was a great house but it was landlocked in one of those gated, guarded communities that were all the rage in south Florida. It was like living in a city-state, everyone in their own private, locked in world.

"Well, I don't know. I don't know where we'll keep it. Maybe we can rent some dock space. People do that, don't they? Or we can keep it in a marina."

Elaine was shaking her head. "A boat! Where on earth did

you ever get such a—" She stopped herself just in time.

But George knew what she was thinking, what she was going to say. *Where on earth did you ever get such a crazy idea?* He smiled. He waited to see how Elaine would recover.

She dug into her noodles. "Well, kids, a boat—won't that be fun!"

George returned to his meal, this time with gusto. In fact, he was surprised how good the food tasted. Elaine's Boca friends had been right, after all.

Who'd have thought?

Elaine was in her cocoon. At least, that's the way George thought of it. She was like one of those Egyptian mummies, all wrapped up, preparing for life in the next world. Buried under the covers, face hidden behind one of those purple silk sleeping masks she favored. She was always too cold. He was always too hot.

George padded across the carpet and flopped down on the bed. Elaine rolled toward her side of the king sized mattress. "I wish you hadn't made fun of me, especially in front of the kids."

Elaine remained silent.

"I mean, was that really necessary?" He pulled the covers up to his chin, turned off the bedside light and let his head hit the pillow, which he punched up with his fists.

"I didn't make fun of you, George," Elaine finally said wearily. "What was I supposed to be making fun of?"

"You made fun of my boat idea."

"No, I didn't."

"Yes, you did. You were ridiculing me."

Elaine rolled onto her back and pulled off her sleep mask. "No, George. I was surprised is all. Surprised that you wanted a boat all of a sudden."

"What do you mean? I've always talked about getting a boat."

His wife sighed. "People talk about a lot of things."

George nodded in the dark. "Well, I want a boat."

"Yes, George." She turned back on her side. "Goodnight. Oh, did you remember your Effexor?"

"Yes, dear." Effexor was the latest wonder drug good old Dr. Grossman had him on. George wasn't sure exactly what it was supposed to do to help him, but he knew what it did to help Doc Grossman, the pharmacist and the pharmaceutical company that made the stuff—it made them all rich—off George's troubles.

Yes, he had remembered it. He'd remembered to flush tonight's tab down the toilet. The Effexor was supposed to help George with his depression. But George wasn't really depressed. No, George was simply crazy. So he'd flushed the drug down the toilet. That way, Dr. Grossman and Elaine couldn't know he wasn't taking his medication. He'd been forced to take it when he was in the hospital both times he'd been institutionalized, the first time for seven days observation and then this last time, when he'd regressed and been sent in for the month.

But they couldn't force him now. Down the toilet it went.

Besides, the stuff made him sleepy and thirsty. Maybe the drug would cheer the commode up some. Because if anyone or anything had the right to be depressed it was a toilet.

—3—

The week leading up to Thanksgiving went by quickly.

Elaine was scurrying about even more than her usual scurrying self and the kids were all excited. It was Thanksgiving vacation and they'd get several days off from school. George promised the kids they could go look for a boat that weekend.

All in all, it hadn't been a bad week. George was even looking forward to Thanksgiving dinner, though he'd have been happier if it had been reserved for his own little family. Nonetheless, he told himself he was going to have a nice time and put a good face on things. Wear his happy face all day and even mean it.

He'd spent that Wednesday afternoon playing eighteen holes of golf with Tim and Claire at the public executive course and was only six over par. After dinner he dozed off in his La-Z-Boy recliner in the den, the morning's paper in his lap. The kids were reading books beside him. Elaine was working away in the kitchen on the morrow's meal.

When he woke, he was alone. His ears tickled. A thin line of sweat fell from the side of his right ear, struck his Adam's apple and rolled under his collar like the touch of a spectral skeleton's thin, bony finger.

The room was dark.

George was scared.

Scared because he had heard something.

Something that scared him not because he didn't know what it was, but because he did.

George thought they were finally gone. But they weren't gone at all.

They were back.

George had told Dr. Grossman they were gone. He'd told Elaine they were gone. And he, himself, had truly believed they were gone.

But were they ever really gone? Could they ever really be gone? The voices?

He pushed the chair back to its upright position. The house was quiet. He looked at his watch but it was too dark to make out the time. Maybe they'd all gone to bed. It was such a big house he couldn't always tell. . .

"George. . .George. . ."

George squirmed in his chair.

"George. . .please. . .please, George. . .come. . .come. . ."

George shook his head though he knew full well that would never make them go away. They never went away, at least not when he wanted. They came and went whenever they wished. And George's wishes didn't matter one bit.

He stood on shaky legs.

"George. . .come now, George. . .help us. . ."

George approached the window and pulled it open. Far away he heard the passing of a small jet. The breeze stirred the tops of the palm trees surrounding the swimming pool. There were lights on in the other wing of the house, the kids' rooms.

George ran.

"George. . .George. . ." pleaded the voices, growing fainter with each stride.

George's hair was all flat on one side and he looked disturbed.

"Are you alright, George?" Elaine was just tucking Claire into bed. Tim was brushing his teeth with one of those electric jobs. Whir-whir-whir.

George kept mum. He couldn't tell anyone about the voices. Not again. "Fell asleep in the chair, that's all."

The kids' rooms were connected by the shared bath and George escaped through the bathroom into Tim's room, avoiding his wife's prying gaze. He thought he heard someone calling his name, hoping it was only the wind passing over the roof and through the trees. Still, he closed Tim's blinds.

George got through the night. Somehow. He'd woken at one a.m., lathered in sweat, the sheets soaked through.

"George, you must come. . .please. . .help. . .help us. . ."

"Dear God," George whispered. He stole out to the kitchen, pulled down a bottle of scotch, drank from the lip, then returned to bed. He stuck his head under the pillow and squeezed it tight.

All the while, the voices pleaded with him. "The ocean. George. . .you must come. . ."

They knew his name. How did they know his name?

"How's George?" whispered Victoria as she stepped into the foyer, carrying a load of sweet potatoes and spinach balls. She was a thin woman with pale skin for a Floridian. Her features were stark as a desert landscape and she'd done her blonde hair up in a tight little bun atop her head.

Elaine looked over her shoulder, looking for George, then said, "Okay, I guess. The doctor says he's better. But he doesn't seem very different."

"Is he still—you know, hearing those voices?" Victoria handed Elaine the dish of spinach balls. "Careful," she said, "they're hot."

Elaine nodded and gingerly accepted the glass dish and carried it into the kitchen. "No, Doctor Grossman says the voices are gone. According to the staff at the hospital, the voices stopped weeks ago."

"That's good," said George's sister. She began unloading the sweet potatoes. Her husband came in with their son, Nick, who was carrying a holiday wreath.

"How sweet," said Elaine. "Hang it on the front door,

will you, Nick?" Nick agreed and attached the wreath to the outside of the door.

"Hello, Nick," said George, coming out of the den. "Spreading some holiday cheer?"

Nick smiled. "Trying. Happy Thanksgiving, Uncle George."

"Gobble, gobble," said George, flapping his elbows. "Ready to eat?"

"Always," answered Nick.

George grinned. "Me, too."

The rest of the clan arrived, George's younger sister, Lorraine and her family, and Elaine's Aunt Emily. George managed to be practically civil to the whole lot of them. Claire, being eight years old, seemed to be having the most fun, he noted. Fun seemed to exist as a geometrical inversion to age.

"Happy Thanksgiving, everyone," George said, carving up the Unturkey. George had never believed in eating meat.

"We should all count our blessings and be grateful for this food," added Lorraine. Her husband, Chuck, who by the look of him had never missed a meal or a donut shop, patted her arm.

George opened the champagne. Elaine played the perfect hostess, being sure everyone, the grownups and the children, were happy and well fed.

Between the second servings and the traditional coffee which would soon work its way round to the traditional desert—pumpkin and pecan pie—George left the table.

Disappeared.

He'd gone without a word and at first no one had noticed. Elaine, on noting his absence, thought he'd probably gone for a glass of water in the kitchen. But when she looked for him there, he was not to be found. That was when she noticed that the sliding glass door at the end of the family room was ajar.

Elaine froze, hearing only the sounds of holiday conversation coming from the dining room. "George?"

She hurried down the hall to their bedroom. Her high heels clicked across the marble tiles like a pair of hungry woodpeckers. She knocked on the bathroom door. "George?"

No reply.

She checked the den and the children's rooms, then the guest bath. No sign of her husband. She hurried back to the dining table and whispered in Tim's ear.

Tim nodded and rose.

"Where's old Georgie?" said Victoria's husband, Danny.

"Bathroom," lied Elaine. She motioned for Tim to get going.

Tim stuck the remaining half of his dinner roll into the corner of his mouth and went out through the family room door, open just like Mom had said. He searched the courtyard. There was no sign of Dad.

"Dad?" he called softly. "Are you out here?" The side gate leading to the backyard was open. "Dad?"

Tim walked completely around the house. There was no

sign of his father. He punched in the code to open the garage doors from the outside. Both cars were there.

For a moment he wondered what he should do. Go back inside and tell Mom he couldn't find Dad? She wouldn't like that. He decided on his second option. He'd take the car and drive around the block. He got the key to the Volvo station wagon off the hook in the hall and backed down the driveway.

He circled around the block. No sign of Dad. Deciding he'd better check the whole neighborhood, Tim drove out in an ever widening circle.

Finally, up past the clubhouse, Tim spotted a familiar figure. It was his father. He recognized the gray suit, the shape of his body and his balding head. His father was walking away, slowly but steadily.

Tim pulled up alongside. He rolled down the window. "Dad. Hey, Dad!"

George walked on. One foot followed the other.

"George. . .George. . .please. . .please, George. . .the ocean. The ocean is waiting for you . . ."

"DAD!" Tim pounded the horn with his fist. Twice, hard.

George stopped. He looked dazed and sweat covered his face like a veil. At first he didn't even look like he'd recognized Tim and Tim wondered if his dad had suffered a stroke. But then, could a guy suffering a stroke be walking around? In the heat?

"Dad?" Tim said softly.

George was staring at him.

25

"George. . .George. . .do not stop now, George. Please, save us. . .save us, George. . ."

Tim took his father's hand. It was cool to the touch though the man looked like he was burning up. He led him around the car and George obediently sat.

"Are you alright, Dad?" A worried look hung in Tim's eyes.

George raised an eyebrow. "Just taking a little walk, son." He patted his stomach and grinned. "You know how it is. I always eat too much on Thanksgiving."

"Yeah, Dad. Me, too."

"Gonna look for a boat tomorrow, eh, son?"

Tim nodded.

"It's going to be great having boat, isn't it, son?"

"Yes, Dad. It'll be great." Tim drove them home.

—4—

There were more types of boats than George had ever imagined.

But none of them spoke to him. They inspected big ones and little ones, climbing up and down the docks and the boats. They looked at big motor cruisers, speedboats and even some sailing ships.

The kids both loved one with twin jet-propulsion, propellor-less engines. The boat could even be controlled by a joystick that looked like it belonged in a video arcade. Stylistically, the motorboat was reminiscent of a lobster boat, the kind George had once watched cruise up and down the coast of Massachusetts the one summer he'd spent there when he was oh-so-much younger.

"Maybe," he said. "We'll see." He patted the toprail affectionately. "We've got more to look at still."

But everybody was tired and Elaine needed to check in on

things at the office, so they left that for another day.

And soon enough, work—type type type—took over like an invisible, invidious parasite and Christmas itself threatened to overwhelm them.

George loved Christmas. It was the one time of year he could buy a bazillion things for Elaine and the kids and she didn't complain he was spoiling them. Last year, the presents had reached halfway up the nearly ten foot Frasier fir.

This year, judging by the size of the pile George was accumulating in his home office, looked to be even better—a record breaker.

But the voices in George's head rose above even the clatter of *Jingle Bells*. And George knew he was mad. Madder than a third generation hatter.

And he didn't know how it had happened. And he wasn't quite sure why it had happened. And he knew for certain that he couldn't tell anyone, not even his wife and especially not Doc Grossman, that it had happened.

They'd just lock him up again. If not in the Miami Institute of Health, then some place like it. And George did not like it.

After all, he was already locked up, wasn't he? Hide behind gray walls, stick little foam thingies in ears, step on boxy gray pedal and type type type. Listen to all the stressed out doctors describing in excruciating detail their patients' ailments.

And this was the busy season, too. Lots of sick patients this time of year. This was partially due to the influx of snowbirds, of course. Down for the winter in sunny Florida. Bringing their aches and pains and depressions with them. Sticking them in George's ears where they lodged like used up chewing gum. Used up chewing gum was gray, too, wasn't it?

And it never came out again.

"George?"

He froze.

"George?" Elaine laid a hand on his chest, rubbing across his pajamas.

George knew what she wanted and he obliged. And the voices kept telling him to come.

Come. . .come. . .come. . .

But he couldn't. Not in any fashion or sense of the word. Elaine did. And he rolled over, pulled up his pajama bottoms and tried to sleep.

Christmas was in three days now. He could last three days now, couldn't he? Couldn't he?

An hour passed by. Then two. He could last. Couldn't he? George had avoided looking at the bedside clock. He looked now. It was one o'clock in the morning.

"George. . ." came the whisper. "Listen, George. . .get the boat, George. . ."

George turned on his side, stuffing the pillow over the used up chewing gum in his ears. He was sweating and cold.

"Come, George. Get in the boat. Get the boat, George. Please. . .George. . ."

George rubbed his neck and then his ears. The voices

were getting louder. They were getting more adamant. Day by day, they had been getting harder and harder to ignore.

"Please, George. We need you. Get in the boat. Get in the boat and come, George."

George sat up.

"Please. Come now, George. . ."

George pricked up his ears. Had the voices stopped?

The wind stirred up the foxtail palm fronds outside his bedroom window. There might be a storm coming up.

George rose to look out the sliding glass door. There weren't too many clouds. Plenty of stars yet and half a moon. Who was sharing the moon tonight? George wondered. Who had the other half?

He went to the bedroom door, punched in the code shutting off the alarm and slipped on his deck shoes. Maybe he'd just step outside for some fresh air.

"Yes, George," called the voices. "There isn't much time. You must, please, help us."

George quietly unlocked the sliding glass door and stepped out onto the courtyard. The air was cool and humid. A scent of chlorine carried from the pool. Tim had bombed it last afternoon.

George stepped to the edge of the pool. It was too dark to see his reflection. He jiggled the car keys in his right hand. Now how did they get there? Had he picked them up off his night table? No matter.

"Come, George. . .we wait for you. . ."

George went to the garage. The big black Mercedes sat

like a sleeping behemoth. Maybe a little drive was what he needed to help him sleep. He got behind the wheel.

He put the key in the ignition. It had been a long time since he'd seen the ocean at night.

Years ago he would even spend all night at the beach with a girlfriend or his buddies. They'd build a little fire out of driftwood and spend the night talking about everything in the universe, life and all its mysteries.

Were there any mysteries left now? It didn't seem like it. And spending all night at the beach was now illegal in Boca. Want to spend the night sitting at the beach, looking at the stars? Lock you up, they will.

George drove towards the ocean.

The voices got louder.

"The boat, George. . .the boat. . ."

He pulled into a small deserted park along the Intracoastal Waterway. The Intracoastal had been built long ago, probably by the Army Corps of Engineers, and ran the length of Florida and then some. He'd heard it even went as far as Washington, D.C. George told the kids that when they got a boat they could take it all the way, searching for the end. Up and back.

Elaine had told him not to do that. Not to get the kids' hopes up like that. After all, how could they take that much time off from work? "Richards Medical Transcription Services doesn't run itself, does it?" she'd said.

No, it did not. But it sure ran them, George was tempted to say. But George had said nothing.

He turned off the engine, left the key in the ignition and got out. He leaned against the warm hood, watching the clouds and the stars. It was like he was in Heaven.

He took a deep breath, taking in the smells of fish and salt. He'd always loved the smell of the ocean and the touch of the ocean breeze on his face.

"George. . .George. . .we are waiting for you, George. . ."

A slight clatter caught George's attention and he walked to the seawall. He gazed at the black waters. There were a couple of small boats moored at a small wooden dock to his left.

"Now, George. . .please, before it is too late. . ."

George examined the small motorboat. There was no key. The little fiberglass rowboat beside it contained two oars. He thought it might be fun to row out into the water a little ways. It wouldn't be wrong, would it? After all, he'd bring the boat back. No one would miss it at this time of night. And it wasn't stealing because he'd be right back.

George climbed inside, struggled to undo the rope, then fell back as the knot slipped loose and the boat lurched away from the dock.

George quickly picked up the oars and began rowing. God, it was peaceful. The sky overhead was dark as all infinity and nothing else seemed to exist. Just George in a rowboat.

He rowed clumsily at first but improved with each stroke.

"George. . .yes, George. . .this way, George. . ."

George followed the voices. The rowing got harder. The

moon got darker. The wind was getting stronger. So were the waves. When he closed his eyes, it was like the tender, invisible hand of infinity was reading his face—his nose, his cheeks, his chin—like a blind woman reaching for his soul.

George had left the Intracoastal now and was out in the Atlantic Ocean. He couldn't believe it! He was rowing in the ocean! He laughed.

"George. This way, George. This way."

And the voices kept calling him. And George kept rowing. He paddled east and the shoreline grew smaller and smaller. His arms grew more and more tired and the oars seemed to get heavier and heavier. His breath was coming out in shorter, shallower, painful little breaths. The shoreline was a distant necklace of twinkling, yellow lights.

"Here, George. Here."

The voices were loud now. Almost shouting.

George stopped rowing. The boat rocked precariously, side to side, in the rollicking waves. He was sweating and his feet were damp from the frigid water which kept splashing into the little rowboat.

The wooden oars were clutched tightly in his hands. His heart was beating like there was a tiny speed metal drummer, deep in his chest, pounding his way to a raucous, climactic finish.

"Now, George. Now."

George stood. There was no one to see him. No one to hear him. "What?" It didn't matter if he talked to the voices now. Elaine wasn't here. Doc Grossman wasn't here. There was no one to call him crazy. No one to take him away for his own good. "What did you say?"

He raised his voice. "Who are you?"

The cool wind whipped through his silk pajamas. He was ill-prepared for this spontaneous sea voyage. Should he go back? Would Elaine wake up and wonder where he'd gone?

He was about to sit back down and pick up the oars when the voices replied.

"We wait for you, George. You must save us."

"What?"

"Save us, George."

George studied the dark sea. The voices seemed to be coming from below. He laughed. He might be crazy, but he didn't believe in mermaids. "Me?"

"Yes, George."

"But—" He stopped. *I'm just a puny little nothing*, he wanted to say. Instead he said. "Why? Why me?"

"Because only you can save us, George."

George stood on unsteady feet, fighting the rocking of the boat, trying to digest these unbodied words. The voices were as crazy as he was!

"Now, George, please. Come."

George leaned over the side. And still he was curious.

"Save us."

George swallowed hard. He thought hard. His hands trembled. George stared at the moving water and the water matched his gaze, staring him down.

He took as deep a breath as he could manage. The

universe itself seemed to hold its breath. Waiting. Waiting for something to happen.

George jumped in.

And he dove. And he dove and he dove and he dove. And he got colder and colder and colder. And the voices called and called and called. And it got darker and darker and darker. And George felt his lungs bursting and his capillaries bursting and his head bursting and then everything was getting light again like his whole mind was exploding.

And George dove and dove and dove. And George knew that he was dying. . .

—5—

"Are you the angels?"

"Angels, George?"

"I hear angels in my head." Why had he suddenly made this admission? After his latest stay in the loonie lab, he'd told himself to deny the voices. Deny they existed. Deny that he heard them. He didn't want Doc Grossman sending him back again, did he? Wait, had Grossman already sent him back?

A cool, comforting hand passed over George's forehead. He could feel it but he couldn't see it. George couldn't see anything. He felt his eyes were open yet all he saw was light. Bright white light. He was lying down. In some sort of bed. He knew that. He was lying down in some sort of soft bed in the center of a star gone nova.

Was Heaven located in the center of a supernova?

Maybe that was it. Right or wrong, it was an answer.

The hand flew away. "Get some rest, George. While there

is yet time."

The voice was airy and feminine just like the angels he'd been hearing. Where was he? Where were the angels?

"Time?"

"Yes, George." The voice came from further away now. "There isn't much time, you know."

George nodded, as if he understood. But George saw nothing and understood even less.

George slept fitfully at first, then drifted off into oblivion. He woke much later, his hands clenching the smooth sheets that covered him. He opened his eyes. Just a crack.

Crack.

There was still an awful lot of light. But not so much as before. George could see now. But he felt as if his head had been split in two like a ripe Crenshaw melon.

He was in a room. Things were hard to make out because, although the room was small, everything looked a bit out of focus, sort of smudgy, as if someone had taken their thumb and rubbed out all the sharp edges, like in a charcoal drawing.

George stared up at a dark blue ceiling. Light crept out of the corners like a chronic leak. Where the hell was he?

He could feel his heart beating in his chest? Did that mean anything? Was he alive? Dead?

George sat up.

Things began to come into focus, as if his eyes and his mind were adjusting to a different sort of reality. Things didn't look quite the way they should, didn't look quite the way he'd remembered them to be, didn't appear the way his mind believed they should be.

A woman came running into the room through an irregularly shaped open doorway, a jagged vulva. Strawberry blonde hair, laced with strands that looked like spun gold, outlined her glowing face and eyes the color of jade took him in. Her features were classic and elegant, her body, clad in a material that looked like some sort of finely fashioned, two-piece animal skin that left her midriff exposed, was well-muscled and seemed to pulse with energy from each and every pore.

George felt suddenly small.

She tossed a knapsack on the bed. "Quickly," she said, pulling away the sheets.

George complained and pulled back.

She tugged the top sheet free. "We must go!"

George felt confused and a little annoyed and more than a little embarrassed, lying there in his wrinkled pajamas, listening to this Amazon of a creature practically ordering him about. "Go? Go where?"

"To rescue the queen, of course." She picked up the knapsack and hefted it in George's face. "There is no time to lose. We must," she repeated adamantly, "go."

George opened his mouth to complain. She practically shoved the backpack in his face. He noted she had a similar one on her own back.

George took the knapsack. It had to weigh a good five kilos. It was made of the same substance as the woman's clothing. She smiled. He wondered again if he was dead or if he was insane and he wondered whether or not it mattered which.

A sharp crack like thunder or God striking the Earth with a baseball bat the size of a small solar system sent the woman running out of the room. "Hurry, George!"

George, clutching the knapsack to his chest, ran after her. "Are you one of the angels?"

"This way!" She twisted along a hall hewn out of solid brown and purple rock, then disappeared from sight. George struggled to get the pack on his back while racing to catch up.

It got darker and darker. George ran alongside his angel. The tunnel became more and more narrow; the ceiling lower and lower. Soon George feared the whole passageway would converge in on itself. What would happen then? Would they shrink and pop out a hole on the other side? Shades of Alice in Wonderland?

They turned sharply and a glow of light ahead cheered George. The angel halted beside a wide underground river whose waters ran quickly into a dark hole in the distance. An alien, metallic odor filled his nostrils. A small dirt path led off in both directions, following the river. Oddly, the river made no sound. It had no voice.

The light appeared to emanate from the rock itself, stronger near the bottom of the cavern walls, then weakening, until it faded away completely overhead.

George paused beside his companion, keeled over and clutched his knees while gasping for breath. His lungs complained. There was something about the air down here that made it difficult to breathe, never mind the twenty minutes or so of trotting. His throat burned. His bare feet, unused to such abuse, were bruised.

The woman turned to George with questioning eyes. George noted that she breathed calmly. Only her slightly disheveled hair gave any evidence that she'd been running at all.

"Which way, George?"

George looked at her in stunned confusion. What the hell was she asking him for? He'd been following her! "What?"

The earth shook with another swing of the bat. God had gotten a piece of it that time. Foul tip!

She leaned in closer, desperation thickened her voice. "Which way?!"

George blustered. "Which way?" He twisted his head. To the left, the river spiraled off into nothingness and the path rose precipitously. To his right, the river turned down through the darkness. The trail was forced to follow suit. Downhill sounded much easier on his feet. And his quavering heart. He pointed toward the right.

She nodded and soundlessly raced down the track.

They passed from the larger cavern into a smaller channel that followed tightly the river's path. There was no light here. The woman carried a small glowing globe in her hand that illuminated the low, damp walls. The river still emitted no sound.

His guide remained silent as well. Only the sounds of

George's panting provided his ears with a reason for being. The smell of the cave had become sulfurous.

Their racing turned into a trot, turning into a jog, notched down to a speedwalk and finally a normal pace, at least for George. They'd traveled downward for what seemed like an hour. George wished he had his watch. The path flattened a little ways and now they were heading upward. George felt as though his lungs had just compressed a year's duty into a couple of hours.

George ran his hand along the cave wall. It was ice cold and wet. He lifted his fingers to his nose in the darkness. Ugh. That was where the sulfur smell originated. Rock sweat.

"*Hait!*" exclaimed George's angel. She held out her arm, dropped the glowing orb into her knapsack and hit the ground.

"What are you—"

She grabbed George by the thigh and pulled him roughly to the ground.

"Look here, what's going on?"

"It is the thing," she whispered.

George didn't know what the 'thing' was but he sure didn't like the way this creature said it. She actually sounded scared! Up until that moment, George wouldn't have thought there was a thing that could even make this wondrous creature bat an eyelash, let alone cringe in fear.

"Listen, you hear the thing?"

George forced himself to stop breathing. He shut his eyes and concentrated. Yes. There was something, almost beyond the range of his ears. But it was growing more distinct. The sound was nearly indescribable; part low howl like a night wind kicking up over the Everglades, with an occasional flap like a sharp wind hitting a mainsail. "Yes," he said quietly. "I hear it."

She held a finger to her lips. "I thought the thing would be gone."

George said nothing. What could he say?

"We must climb." George's angel rose and grabbed at the wet rock. In half a second she was a good couple of meters up.

George admired her ability.

"Hurry, George!" She held onto the rough stone with only her feet and one hand as she motioned in the near blackness for George to follow her.

"But, I can't—" The sound was getting louder. A howl, rumble, rumble, rumble. Snap!

"George!"

George grabbed the rock and pushed himself upward. He managed to get one foot off the ground before falling back.

"George!"

The sound grew louder.

George tried again. His wet foot slipped on the rock wall. It was impossible to climb. How the hell had she managed it? His hands fumbled in the dark and he found purchase. He pushed himself up with all his strength, found a tiny crevice for his right foot and pushed himself up some more. Twice more he ascended. The woman was a good five meters up by now and waiting.

There was a sharp snap and the tiny cave grew brighter. A sweet smell, like a truckload of overripe bananas rotting on the docks of Port Everglades, assaulted his nostrils. George dangled by his hands, unable to find support for his feet as the thing passed below. He willed his legs to stop moving. They weren't listening.

The angel motioned for him to remain silent. She didn't have to tell George twice.

Straining to peer over his right shoulder, he saw the thing. It was thick and squat with oily black skin. Two toadish eyes gave its head a camelback appearance. Its nose stuck out like a blackened tree stump. Around its huge neck was an orb, thrice the size of the one the woman carried, attached to a braided rope.

It walked on two massive legs and was shaped like a flattened pear. Its mouth hung open and it breathed loudly. When its mouth slammed shut there came the snapping sound that George had now grown familiar with.

Massive as the thing was, it managed to walk sideways along the trail. Apparently it was used to such inconveniences.

The thing had stopped right under George; its sweet breath rising in a mist that threatened to engulf them both. George thought he was going to be sick. Would the thing mind if he threw up on it?

The eyes moved like a crow's as it would stalk a lizard or a grasshopper, in sharp darting motions. The globose eyes, milky ooze with no discernible irises, looked at the river. They looked up the trail and down. Then they looked up at George. George turned his face back to the cave wall, shut his eyes and held his breath. Please, please, please, he thought, don't let that damn thing see me.

—6—

The thing paused, appeared to be watching and thinking.

Rasp, rasp, snap! With a deep cry, it threw itself at the cave wall. The rock shook and George's left hand slipped. The thing was trying to knock him down!

George opened his eyes and reached for a small outcropping overhead. His fingers grabbed sharp stone that tore cruelly at his flesh.

The thing hit the wall again. The vibrations resonated through George's teeth and bone. His right hand gave out. George's right foot, not expecting the extra load, followed suit.

He was falling!

The angel reacted quickly. She grabbed George under the shoulders and held him suspended, gritting her teeth and struggling to hold them both off the ground.

George looked down. The thing's eyes swivelled madly.

It emitted a high-pitched whine resembling a car engine being pushed to and over its limits. George wondered what the thing would try next.

Then there was a smacking sound as it pulled its oily black body from the rock wall. The three of them hung there for a moment, locked into a shared frame of time and space, and then the thing picked up one of its overlarge legs and put it down again. A few minutes later the thing and its sounds were out of sight, heading up the path that George and his angel had taken.

The smell of overripe bananas lingered.

George fell to the ground. The angel wasn't far behind though she came far more gracefully.

"What was that?" he whispered hoarsely.

"That was the thing." With no further words nor explanation, she pulled her own light orb from her pack and resumed her march.

George would have complained but he was afraid to speak more—afraid the thing would hear him, supposing it had ears with which to do so, and would return. George pushed himself up to his feet. His hands were covered with sticky black goo. So were his pajama bottoms.

And it stunk.

Time stopped working. And so George gave up on it. Why cling to a concept that had no more use and apparently no further validity? Time, and Reality itself, had become as useful to George as a mateless sock with a fat hole in the big toe.

The stench of overripe, fly-ridden bananas faded into a memory—a memory George wished he could erase from his hippocampus or wherever the hell that particular memory was stored.

With the smell all but gone, George stopped dwelling on the 'thing'. He also stopped getting these preposterous thoughts that Carmen Miranda, with a plate of rotten fruit on her head, was going to be coming dancing around the next turn or the turn after that. Perhaps begging him to dance.

He turned his attention back to where he was and the angel he was with. Where were they going?

To save the queen? What the hell did that mean?

Elaine woke. Something felt wrong. Something was wrong. "George?" Her hands searched for her husband in the darkness and came up empty.

She pulled off her silk sleep mask and sat up in the bed. The curtains were partially open. The sliding glass door was ajar and the breeze whipped up the bottom of the fine white draperies which danced like a haunted southern belle seeking her long lost dance partner.

She stood and padded barefoot across the floor. She stuck her head out the open slider. All was quiet. She stepped out. "George?"

—7—

They crawled through a slick, rough hole of rock that gave George the willies. What if there was a cave-in? He shivered.

They'd be buried alive, that's what.

George didn't like small, tight spaces. George didn't like dark places. This place was small, tight and dark. A triple threat.

And it was cold.

He paused to catch his breath. Crawling along on his belly in his pajamas was difficult. He closed his eyes and hoped he'd wake up at home, in bed, when he opened them again.

George counted to twenty. Twice. He ever so slowly opened his right eye. He wasn't in bed. It hadn't worked. There was no extra firm mattress, no contouring foam pillow. No wide screen TV beckoning him with its potential of electron soup.

He looked up. The angel had disappeared in the darkness. Hell! George pushed himself forward, with only his hands to guide him. He thought he saw a glimmer of light ahead and moved faster.

"Oooph!" George fell on his stomach, hard. His ribs took the brunt of the blow. He pushed ahead. He couldn't move. He was stuck.

"Hey!" he called. "Hey!" George's heart was racing. He was alone, trapped in a dark crawlspace under a mountain somewhere!

George twisted to the left, barely moving ten centimeters. He tried turning the other way and found it impossible. It was his knapsack. It had become lodged between himself and the rock.

He was sweating. Damn! He should have removed the pack as the cave narrowed. Why hadn't she warned him to remove it?

He shouted. "Help!" The sound seemed to soak into the rock. Would she hear? Would she return when she noticed George wasn't following?

He planted his palms in the hard ground and tried to pull himself forward. God, he was going to die here. Alone. George strained with all his might, gasped and collapsed. He hadn't budged at all.

George collected his wits and tried again. This time he'd try pushing backwards. He was able to get his knees bent, just barely. He pushed back. The knapsack slipped.

"Yes," he grunted. He pushed again. The pack slipped

some more.

Energized, George gave it his all. The strap of the backpack tore loose and the pack shifted up his back, lodging between his neck and shoulders tighter than ever. George's face was pushed down to the ground, twisted sharply to the side, one ear planted in the ground.

He cried out, his jaw straining against the rocky floor. There was nothing more he could do. He was going to die here—wherever 'here' was. Was he in Hell? Would he wake up and do it all over again? This whole crazy adventure? Like Sisyphus? Was he doomed to an existence in an infinitely relived nightmare?

George shut his eyes and tried to will himself smaller. Maybe once he'd been lying here long enough, he'd become dehydrated enough that he'd be able to squeeze out—if he had the energy left to move at all. . .

Funny, the cold, dark, silent tomb he was encased in was even more frightening to him than that impossible monster they'd encountered earlier. Scarier even than being locked up in Grossman's loonie lab.

He thought about his children, Tim and Claire. Was it morning? Were they awake? What about Elaine? Did she know he was gone now?

When she did notice, what would she think? She'd think he'd run away, probably. She'd think he'd lost his mind. Poor Elaine. You don't know where I am and neither do I.

George felt himself slipping away. Was he running out of oxygen?

"George!"

A sharp blow glanced over the top of George's skull and the knapsack was pulled free. Hands urged him forward. "Come, George. Please, please, George, come."

George heard voices. They were angel voices. He didn't want to see them. He didn't want to hear them.

The hands tugged at his hands and he fought them off. "No," he said. "No."

"Please, George. Please. Come, George. There is so little time."

George, surrendering to his fate, realizing that the angels might leave him stuck there in that tomblike hole, opened his eyes and gripped the helping hands. It was her. She pulled him forward. Soon he was able to move on his own.

In the narrow quarters, the angel was forced to crawl backwards. There wasn't room to turn around. A triangular light ahead gave George heart and he quickened. She wormed her way out of the horrible little tunnel and George hurried after her.

He didn't want to be alone in that fearful place ever again.

They were in a desert with a sky of orange and blue. Two dead brown trees stood, one on each side of the slim cave entrance, keeping eternal watch.

The heat was oppressive, yet it felt oddly humid. George looked up and winced. The unfiltered light hurt his eyes. There wasn't a cloud in sight. George sampled the air. It smelled salty. Like maybe they were standing on a long dry ocean bed.

The angel grabbed his left hand and frowned. "We'd better attend to that." She dropped George's hand. "Sit."

George squatted and examined his hand. The fingertips were shredded and a long, jagged gash cut diagonally across his palm. "Who are you?"

The woman knelt beside him and opened her knapsack. After a moment's rummaging she brought out a small tube of paste. "Enjoy the sting." She squeezed out a line of brown goo and rubbed it into George's hand.

He grimaced. Tears came to his eyes. Enjoy the sting? What sort of a sadist was this creature? Was she an angel or one of the Devil's minions?

"I am Cleea." She screwed the cap back on the white tube and dropped it into her pack. "Thank you for coming, George." She stood and slipped her pack back over her shoulders. "We'd better get moving."

George reluctantly got to his feet. Every part of him was in pain. His lungs felt as if they were being dangled on a pair of sharpened live oak sticks over a low, white hot campfire—the air itself was as hard to breathe here as it had been in the confines of the cave.

The bottoms of his feet were swollen. His knees and elbows were bruised from crawling around in the dark. His hands were in ruins from trying to climb away from that weird thing in the cavern. His ribs ached from falling and his head throbbed from where this angel had punched him in an effort to dislodge his pack.

The angel, Cleea—was that her name or her species?—was looking at him.

George stood nervously, shifting his weight side to side, trying to find some comfortable, or at least less uncomfortable, way of standing. Still she stared at him. "What?"

"Which way?"

"Huh?"

"Which way, George?"

"Which way?" George swivelled. Again, which way? This was madness. This Cleea was even crazier than he was!

Behind them was a rocky morass, occupying a full forty degrees of the panorama. Everything else was desert. And there was lots of it. George wondered how far away the horizon was here. Only one way to find out.

He pointed at an imaginary spot on a line that began just to the left of the cave mouth and ended somewhere in the blurry distance, if it ended at all. "That way."

Hey, if she was crazy enough to ask him, what the hell, he'd oblige and give her an answer. Nobody was going to out-crazy old George.

The woman nodded solemnly and marched off, unquestioningly, in the direction he had indicated.

George shook his head and took a lingering last look at the cave from which he'd only just escaped. Was it his link to his past life, his real life in Boca Raton, Florida? If so, would he ever see the cave or his home again?

The Cleea creature had shrunken to half-size now in the

distance. George headed after her. His bare feet sank in the soft, desert sand with each hurried step. The loose, fluid sand was as warm as tepid bath water. At least his hand had ceased aching.

"Hey! Hey, Cleea!" George ran the last few steps, coming up abreast the angel. She slackened her pace and smiled. It was the first time George had seen her smile. "So," he said, "is Cleea your name, or. . ."

"Cleea is my name, George."

"And when you said 'thank you for coming'—" With effort, George managed to match his step with hers.

She laid a gentle hand on his upper arm, without losing stride. "I meant it." Her eyes met his. "Thank you, George."

She seemed so serious, so genuine, that George could only nod. "You're welcome." But for what, he did not know.

He had no idea what they were talking about. He had no idea where they were going—and this Cleea was following him!

Heaven help them both.

—8—

It was like walking inside a planet-sized, hot sand covered furnace. George's clothing—pajamas meant for no stronger a travail than a tussling with his wife for the bedcovers—were in tatters. His face burned.

George's lips were dry and cracked. His tongue felt as if Andre the Giant had stomped on it. And the walking continued. Step after step after numbing step.

Didn't this Cleea ever stop? Didn't she ever drink?

The light had grown intolerable and George's seared eyes throbbed painfully. He kept his injured hand glued to his brow like a visor as they passed up a sloping sand dune that grew softer underfoot as they climbed.

Cleea, a half dozen steps ahead, stopped at the summit, gazing into the unseeable distance. Huffing and puffing with relief, George drew up at her side.

George's foot slipped in the liquid brown sand and he

cursed, his heart beat wildly. Inches away, the dune dropped off severely, a sheer rocky fall ending in a broad, boulder littered beach and an unending sea.

Cleea caught him by the arm to steady him. "Careful, George."

George nodded. Careful, indeed. The sand dune stretched out to either side. The precipice had to be a good thirty meters. What was she going to do next? Fly?

Maybe, if she was an angel.

George stepped away from the edge, watching Cleea, wondering if she would sprout puffy, white wings. "At least there's water."

"Water?"

George pointed toward the unfamiliar sea.

"Yes. To drink, I hope."

"You are thirsty, George." She spoke plainly, without taking her eyes from the sky.

"Yes, I'm thirsty! Aren't you?"

Cleea shrugged. "There is no time now. Look." She raised a sinuous arm and pointed to a dark smudge between the edge of the sea and the sky.

"No time? When will there be time? When we've both collapsed from dehydration?" George kicked the sand in frustration. "And how are we going to get down there, where the water is, anyway?"

"Look, George."

George sighed. "Fine. I'm looking," he said with a complete lack of interest and civility. He folded his arms. The smudge had gotten large. "What am I supposed to be looking at?"

"Don't you see that dark spot? It is an arkan, is it not, George?" Her brow was furrowed with worry.

"An arkan?" George watched the gray smudge as it closed the distance between itself and the cliff's edge. It was growing larger and darker. Soon it was apparent that this was some sort of flying creature—a wild, crazy, dinosaur of a bird, with deep blue feathers and piercing yellow eyes. Its sharp, webbed feet were bright red, as if they'd been dipped in fresh blood. An all too real possibility, in George's opinion.

"Quickly, George! I believe she has spotted us!" Cleea threw herself to the ground and began digging into the sand, quickly covering her legs with earth. "Hurry, George. She's come from across the Zephrinzee. The arkan will be hungry."

Hungry? George fell to the ground and pushed sand up over his legs and torso.

"We must bury ourselves. Lie still, George." Sitting beside him, Cleea pushed George's head down. "I will cover you and then myself."

"Wha—" George spat as two fistfuls of desert sand hit him in the face, biting into his eyes and clogging his nostrils and mouth with silt.

"Lie still!"

A large shadow replaced the harsh desert light. The bird was huge; its wingspan enormous. It circled them like a lazy B-52. George squeezed his eyes shut as Cleea buried him alive.

"Do not move until the arkan is gone," Cleea whispered.

George, too scared to even nod, lest it dislodge the sand that covered him head to toe, wondered just how they were supposed to know when the bird-beast was gone when they couldn't even see it.

Come to think of it, he wondered after a few quick and painfully unsuccessful efforts, how were they supposed to breathe?

—9—

Tim sat up, rubbed his eyes and pushed a lock of hair from his forehead.

In the faint light showing through the blinds he could just make out the time. Six-thirty. He groaned. Christmas vacation and instead of sleeping in, Mom was up at the crack of dawn, again. He could hear her working in the kitchen, grinding fresh roasted beans for the coffee, cutting up fruit for their breakfast.

He threw on a t-shirt and quietly opened the door to the bathroom that connected his room to Claire's. She was curled up like a cat. He shook her gently. "Time to get up, Claire."

She sat up. "I'm still tired." As if to prove her point, she yawned.

"So am I, but you hear Mom out there. She'll be calling for us."

"I'm going back to bed." She pulled the covers up to her

ears.

Tim sighed. "Suit yourself." What the heck, Mom would make her get up soon enough.

He left through Claire's room. Their mother was hovering over the kitchen sink. At the sight of her across the counter, Tim was startled. She was still in her bathrobe! This time of day she was normally showered and dressed for the office.

He approached cautiously, his kid radar up to full power. "Morning, Mom," he said, speaking tentatively.

"Oh!" Mrs. Richards looked up in surprise. "It's you, Timmy. You startled me." She shut off the faucet. "Good morning."

Timmy? She hadn't called him that since he was twelve. Tim went around the bar and gave his mother a hug, a kiss on the cheek. Her eyes were puffy and red. "You okay?"

"Yes, yes. I'm fine." She ran a hand through his hair. "Is your sister up?"

"Sort of." Tim opened the fridge, studied its contents, and pulled a red apple from the bin. His mother had prepared sliced peaches. Not his favorite. He rinsed the apple under the sink, dried it on his shirt and took a bite. It was cold and tart. "Where's Dad?"

"Dad?"

"Yeah, you know. Brown eyes, dark brown hair, receding hairline, about this tall." Tim held up a hand. "He lives with us."

"He-he's at the office."

"Already?" Dad never went to the office early. He hated

going at all, let alone early. "How come?"

"How come! How come because he did, that's how come. Now sit down and eat your breakfast! You think I don't have anything better to do than to argue with you?" Mrs. Richards collapsed against the edge of the sink.

"Are you okay, Mom?"

Mrs. Richards managed a weak smile. "Yes, I'm sorry, Tim. Please, take care of your sister for me, will you? I-I have some things to attend to."

Tim looked puzzled. "Sure, Mom. Sure."

"That's a boy. I'll be back soon." She snatched her purse from the ledge by the phone and grabbed her car keys. "You and Claire start breakfast and I'll be right back. I promise."

"It's okay. I can handle things."

Mrs. Richards nodded, went down the hall, opened the door leading to the garage and called out for Claire to get up and eat breakfast. "And you listen to your brother, you hear me?"

Tim heard Claire shout yes. The garage door closed. "Wow," he muttered. "Mom's flipped. I've never seen her go out in her bathrobe before!"

Tim called Claire to come out. As he waited, he got to thinking. He picked up the phone and called his parents' office. It rang and rang and finally the machine kicked in. Tim waited for the taped recording to run its course. "Dad? Dad? Are you there?"

Tim held the phone to his ear, hoping his father would pick up. He didn't. It wasn't unusual for his father not to answer the phone, in fact, it was typical. He never answered the phone, particularly at the office. He didn't want anyone to know he was there. But Tim couldn't help wondering why his dad didn't answer after hearing his voice. . .

He hung up and dialed again.

Sharp talons clawed the earth. The giant bird was after him. George felt like a doppelganger Janet Lee, fighting for his life in a fantastic Hitchcockian horror film.

Though in this case there was no real fight to be fought. And there was nowhere to run even if he had chosen to do so. George didn't bother to hold his breath because he had no breath left to hold. All he could do was lie there and let the beast try to dig him out.

So lie there is all he did, hands clenched. Body tight.

The claws struck his cheeks and he cried out.

"George!"

Fingers swept the dirt from his eyes.

"George. Please, come. There is no time."

George opened his eyes. Cleea leaned over him, her red-gold hair shining like a halo around her angelic face. Dear God.

"Come, George."

She held out a hand and George clasped it. The heavy sand fell away as she helped him to his feet and he felt almost buoyant.

George quickly scanned the sky. It was empty. Cleea stooped at the edge of the cliff and began sweeping aside the

sand which cascaded to the beach far below. George watched
with interest. He didn't relish marching further along this
waterless desert and he wasn't about to jump to his death.

Nor was he interesting in sticking around up here on the
cliff, a sitting duck for the next arkan with an empty belly to
come along.

Soon, Cleea had cut a two meter swath of sand away from
the edge, exposing gray rock. She muttered, slapped her
thighs and rose. "No, this is no good." She paced the edge,
found another spot that apparently suited her and dropped to
her knees. In a matter of minutes she'd uncovered another
stretch of rock.

Cleea grunted with satisfaction and removed her pack.
From within, she removed a slender rope, no wider than a
stick of licorice. She attached this to a nub of rock no larger
than George's hand.

She stood and gave the rope a tug. "That shall do nicely."

George stepped back. She wasn't expecting them to climb
down on that, was she?

She hurled the bulk of the rope over the side. George
heard it slap against the sharp rocks, then all was quiet.

Cleea leaned over, gripped the thin rope with both hands
and leaped over the side. "Hurry, George!"

Her voice carried up over the cliff, giving George a chill.
She was gone! He turned around. The desert offered no
solace. Still, maybe if he waited until nightfall—was there a
nightfall in this crazy place?—and traveled slowly, he could
find his way back to the cave and back to that room and. . .

And what?

What if he couldn't find the cave? The desert looked the same in every direction. Would he be able to follow their previous footsteps? Would he see them in the dark? Would he see the cave?

And then he'd have to crawl through that tight space again—that tight, little space where he couldn't breathe and he couldn't move and his mind stopped working and he had almost died.

He shook himself. And that banana-breath thing might be in there. Could he get past it? It almost killed him the first time. What tricks might it have up its sleeve given a second chance at the job?

And if he survived and when and if he found the room where he'd awakened, what would he next do? If he laid back down in that bed and closed his eyes, would he wake up at home, in Boca Raton?

Or would he merely wake up in that crazy room? George didn't want to end up in a crazy room. Not that crazy room, not any crazy room.

He'd been there before.

Cautiously, George approached the cliff side. He was afraid of heights. He forced himself to look down.

Cleea waved up at him. "Hurry, George!"

George swallowed and the walls of his throat came together like sheets of scratchy sandpaper. There was lots of water down there.

He put a tentative hand on the rope and gave it a tug. It

felt smooth and rubbery in his fingers. The rock it was attached to looked so small. Still, it had held her. It should hold him, too, shouldn't it?

He tugged again and took a deep breath. George dropped carefully to his knees—it wouldn't do to fall over the side now—and grabbed the rope as tightly as he could. His left hand, cut up in the cave, howled in pain.

"Hurry, George! There is no time!"

Jesus, George was getting sick of hearing that! He pushed his legs out behind him and gasped as they fell over empty space. "Ugh!"

His arms jerked tightly in his shoulder sockets. Unable to see, George felt around with his toes for a hold. There was none. He was going to have to use his hands alone.

Slowly, fist after fist, George inched lower. Pausing to catch a breath, he glanced down. Halfway, he thought, I'm nearly halfway.

He continued downward. Something dripped down on his forehead. "What the hell?"

George kept on. There was another drip. George looked up at the rope. The wound on his left hand had opened up again. The rope was getting slippery.

George quickened his pace. His left hand throbbed with pain and soon he was half falling, half sliding down the rope. He tried to slow and stabilize himself with his right hand but managed only to grip a slick spot of blood.

And George was falling. Fast. He screamed and was bounced against the cliff face like a broken ragdoll.

The rope suddenly pulled out, catching him between the legs. He hit the ground with a belly-flop.

"George?"

George couldn't move. George couldn't breathe. All the air had been knocked out of him. His arms and legs were splayed. He was an upside down snowangel.

He pushed wet sand from his mouth with his tongue. Two hands reached down, hooked him by the shoulders and lifted him to his knees.

"I pulled the rope away from the rocks so you wouldn't get hurt." Cleea dusted off his shirt.

"Gee, thanks," muttered George, teetering on his knees, fighting to get his eyes into focus.

–10–

"Is this all there is?" Elaine Richards asked.

The officer nodded. "I'm afraid so, ma'am." He held open the car door while Mrs. Richards looked inside.

It was George's Mercedes alright, with the car key still in the ignition. The keyring was the one that Claire had made for her father in school, with beads and string. It was a red and yellow dragonfly. George said he loved it. So why would he leave it?

Why would he leave everything?

Elaine pulled back from the car and wrapped her arms around herself. Dear God, she hoped nothing bad had happened to George. What if he had been mugged? Or worse, killed?

The detective, with the slack jaw and a row of uneven stubble who'd first introduced himself returned from questioning an elderly boater over by the docks. "Was your husband having any personal problems, Mrs. Richards?"

The question took her by surprise. How should she answer? She didn't feel like telling this stranger about her husband's problems. "No," she said, refusing to look the young man in the eye. "None at all." She turned to the uniformed officer. "Can't you find him, please?"

The detective answered. "We've filed a missing persons report. There is no sign of foul play."

"How can you be sure?" Elaine wondered.

"Well," said the detective, pulling a tiny box of chewing gum from his pocket, "there is no evidence of a struggle. And no bits of hair or blood." He juggled the sugar coated rectangle in his hand before popping it into his mouth and biting down.

"Blood?" Elaine gasped. Her face paled.

"Now, now," said the uniformed officer. "Don't you worry, Mrs. Richards. I'm sure your husband will turn up. He's probably out taking a stroll."

The officer looked up at the sky. "It's a beautiful morning for it." He offered her the gum. She shook her head no and he pocketed the open pack.

"But the car keys—"

"Maybe he simply forgot them. Is your husband a forgetful guy? I mean, I know I forget things all the time. The wife is always getting on me about it."

"Well, I-I suppose." Elaine looked at the Intracoastal, watching a motor yacht cruise lazily past.

"There you go." The detective took Mrs. Richards' arm.

"You go on home. Your husband may be there right now. If he is, you give us a call. Officer Clark here will drive the Mercedes back for you."

Elaine nodded obediently. "Yes, thank you." She returned to the Volvo and waited for Officer Clark to turn the Mercedes around. Where was George?

"What did the old guy say?" Officer Clark asked the detective.

"Not much. Been here since dawn and hasn't seen anything."

"Hmmm." Officer Clark climbed into the Mercedes and settled into the large, comfortable seats. Man, some guys had all the luck.

"Said a little rowboat was missing. Probably some kids."

"Yeah. Nobody would trade a new Benz for an old rowboat. A guy would have to be nuts."

Officer Clark closed the car door and turned the air conditioner down to seventy-two degrees. The Mercedes had four zone air conditioning and GPS. Yes, some guys had all the luck.

George fought his way to the water's edge. The beachsand was soft and wet. His feet sank to his ankles with each difficult step. At least he didn't seem to have any broken bones. He looked back at the deadly cliff face and considered his relatively unscathed condition a miracle.

He lowered his hands to the water. It was relatively warm

and the waves lackluster. He cupped his hands together and brought them to his dry, cracked lips.

"No, George!"

Cleea slapped his hands apart, sending bits of his life's blood in every direction, or so it appeared to George.

"What's the matter with you?"

"It's no good, George. You know that." She turned her back on him and marched out into the surf, stopping when it reached her waist. She splashed her face and leaned backwards, dipping her hair until it was soaking wet and then wringing long strands out using both hands.

Cleea turned back to shore, her golden hair clinging to her golden skin. Once more, George could only think of her as an angel. She stood, looking in George's direction, the water rising halfway up her well-shaped calves.

She was looking at him. Before she could speak, George pointed up the shore to the right; knowing that she would ask him which way.

Cleea nodded curtly and lifted her legs, veering towards the beach as she marched ahead. With longing, George looked at the ocean of water before him, apparently undrinkable, and stumbled after his angel like a lost apostle.

They wandered this way for some time. The cliff, gray and black, loomed above them. Boulders the size of Volkswagens littered the beach.

There appeared to be no tide, as the waves reached the shoreline in more or less the same spot each time. There were few shells and those George saw were broken; some with tiny holes drilled in their sides as if they'd been attacked by conchs.

Though there was still no sign of a sun, it did appear to be growing darker; subtly at first, a little gray around the edges, until the air seemed filled with bits of gray matter that soaked up the light.

Up ahead, what George took for a large, oblong rock half-submerged in the sea from a distance, became a slick olive green as they neared.

It looked to be a turtle of some sort—though like nothing on earth that he'd ever seen—it was as large as an army tank. Its long, rounded head stuck out like a thick turret. A slow wheeze escaped its gaping mouth, as though it were fighting off a bad case of pulmonary edema.

"Good work, George."

"What?"

Cleea strode straight up to the beast while George stayed off to the side. The waves rode up over the edges of the creature's leathery carapace.

The beast's eyes looked rheumy, with a milky white substance oozing out from the sides of the eye orbits. Its neck hung weakly, and the giant turtle barely moved, barely acknowledged their presence.

Cleea smiled warmly and pressed a hand to the creature's nose. She closed her eyes and nodded.

George felt sorry for the big turtle. She was obviously ill. Maybe they could help her. Maybe something positive could come from all this. He'd always felt an affinity for animals. That's why he'd chosen vegetarianism as a way of life.

Forgetting his own troubles, George took a step toward Cleea and the unwell sea creature. "Is there anything we can do to—"

Cleea opened her eyes, glanced quickly at George, nodded once more to the sick turtle. She rubbed its nose tenderly. George came closer. Perhaps they could clean its eyes. Get it some food. He wondered what sort of diet the creature preferred.

But that was not to be. Before he could react, Cleea had raised her left arm. "*Hai!*" Her stiff hand came down in a blur between the creature's unwavering eyes. Two sharp chops and the turtle's head fell dead to the sand.

"Hey!" George raced to the turtle's side. Its eyes had closed. He held a hand over its nostrils. There was no more sign of breathing. "What did you do that for?"

"I put her out of her misery. She was dying, you know, George."

"And so you just—"

"Just what?" Cleea looked quite confused.

"Just hit her like that." George crossed his arms and looked at her with disgust.

Cleea shrugged, lifting her short skirt and extracting a long and sharp white-handled knife. Its edge was serrated, slightly hooked, and vicious looking. George stepped back. Was he about to be next?

"She was dying, George. Suffering. No one should

suffer."

George stifled a bitter response. He'd been suffering for what seemed like an eternity and she hadn't seemed to mind that too much. "You didn't have to do it that way."

"It was the best way that I could, George." She tightened her grip on the knife handle. "Tell me, how could I have done better?"

She actually sounded like she wanted to know. "I-I don't know," George confessed. He stabbed the sand with his foot. The turtle's neck was sinking into the wet ground, as if the earth would swallow the creature up, taking it to another world, perhaps one beneath this crazy one where they now stood.

"Besides, it is what she wanted."

"What she wanted?" George said slowly.

Cleea nodded. "Yes, George. How else would we get across the Zephrinzee and she to Heaven?"

"Heaven?" George bent his neck and looked up at the darkening sky. Was Heaven a place up there somewhere? If he had a telescope, could he locate it? Would he be there soon?

Cleea took off her pack and set it atop a flattish, blue-black rock several yards clear of the water's edge. Returning to the dead creature, she ran a hand along its side. Her other hand held the knife.

She fell to her knees in the water beside the beast and probed some more. Seeming satisfied, Cleea moved her knife from her right hand to her left and placed it against the giant turtle's shell, where the carapace met the plastron. With one hand on the knife's grip and the other on the butt of the knife's handle, she pushed.

As Cleea worked the blade side to side, it slowly penetrated to the hilt. She removed it slowly and started all over again.

Yellowish ooze leaked from the dead turtle's side, like pale egg yolk. The smell was ghastly, like molten black tar mixed with rancid Gruyere cheese.

George turned away, clutching his nose. He doubled over, vomiting up nothing and gagging on his own bitter bile. Hands on knees to steady himself, he forced himself to turn his head.

Cleea was prying the beast's shell apart. Her hands, slathered in dead turtle body fluids, pulled with all their strength. The crack grew wider. Cleea picked up her knife and began poking more holes in the shell.

Collecting his mind and his dignity, George splashed through the water to her side. The smell was overwhelming and he forced himself to take small, shallow breaths. "So, what's this supposed to be? Dinner?"

"George!"

The tone of Cleea's voice was one of shock and disappointment. In fact, it sounded just like one of Elaine's list of Georges.

George scanned his memory. Yes, it most closely resembled George Number 19, page 2, line 3. *George, how could you say such a thing?!*

She turned back to her work, sawing vigorously between the holes she'd created in the dead turtle's underside. It was slow work, but the creature's carapace was rubbery, not bone hard. And she was making steady progress.

Like a scolded schoolboy, George turned, shoulders bent, and headed slowly back to the beach. He perched on the rock beside Cleea's pack, feeling as if he'd misbehaved or misspoken and he didn't know how or why.

Dejectedly, he watched as Cleea worked her way around the beast. Soon she was in deeper water and in back of the turtle, out of his sight completely.

George felt all alone. Just himself and an impossible looking, giant dead sea turtle. Both of them sitting beside a giant, impossible sea.

George wondered. Was he dead, too?

−11−

"Where have you been?" Tim rose from the sofa. He was in his pajama bottoms and t-shirt. "There have been like a million phone calls for you, Mom."

"I had some business. Why aren't you in school, Tim?"

"School?" Tim's face scrunched up in disgust. "This is Christmas vacation!"

Mrs. Richards blushed. "Oh, that's right. Where's your sister?"

Tim shrugged. "Playing in her room, I guess." He looked at his mother who was still wearing her housecoat. "Uh, Mom, aren't you going to the office?"

"The office?"

"Yeah. I mean, like I said, there must have been a dozen calls for you from the employees looking for you." He took a step towards his mother. "Is everything okay?"

Mrs. Richards grabbed a cup of cold coffee from the

counter and drank quickly. Her hand was shaking. "Of course everything is okay. It's hectic this time of year, is all. I'm sure your father is handling things at the office just fine."

Right, thought Tim. Dad would be sequestered away in his gray little corner of the office ignoring every thing and avoiding everybody. He wouldn't even pick up the telephone!

"I'm going to get showered and changed." She looked at the clock. "Oh, dear. It is late." She ran down the hall to the master bedroom.

When she reappeared, she looked more like her usual self, to Tim's relief.

"You two will be okay while I'm at the office, won't you?"

"Yes, Mom." Tim was in the bathroom, brushing his teeth. He spat into the sink. He looked at his mother's reflection in the big mirror over the vanity that extended the entire width and ran all the way up to the ceiling. "What time is Dad going to be home? Early?"

Tim knew his dad liked to come home pretty early, especially when he and Claire were off from school and Tim always looked forward to spending the extra time with him. Maybe they could go bowling.

"I'm not sure, Timmy," Mrs. Richards replied, rummaging in her purse for her keys. "He-he has some errands to run, so don't get your hopes up."

Timmy? There she goes calling him Timmy again!

Mrs. Richards patted him on the head, and pushed open the door that connected the bathroom to Claire's room.

Claire sat on the edge of her bed reading.

Claire looked up. "Hi, Mommy."

"Hi, baby." Mrs. Richards gave her little girl a kiss. "Mommy has to go to the office for a while."

"Can I come?"

"No," said Mrs. Richards, stooping down to her daughter's level. "It would be terribly boring for you. You stay home and play with Tim, okay?"

"Tim doesn't want to play." Claire crossed her little arms and pouted.

"Tim," called Mrs. Richards, "please, play with Claire, would you?"

"Okay, Mom," answered Tim, as he tried sweeping his hair left to right then, dissatisfied, tried combing right to left.

After she'd gone, Tim picked up the telephone. He dialed the office. "Hello? Dad? Can you hear me?" Tim held his breath, waiting. There was no reply. "Well, if you can hear me, I just want to let you know that Mom's on the way. Okay?"

He pressed his ear tightly to the receiver. Nothing but the sound of the machine running and his own quiet breathing. Then he heard a tiny clicking sound. "Dad?" Nothing.

He hung up.

Cleea trudged up out of the water and woke George.

George, who had fallen asleep, lying in the sand, his head against the rock, opened his eyes warily. It was dark. Something like stars hung in the sky.

There was no moon.

"What's going on?"

"Are you hungry, George?"

"Are you kidding?" He felt like he hadn't eaten in about a century. He sat up.

The angel stuck her hand in her pack, rummaged around and brought out a small tight bundle. From this, she removed a finger-thick, rectangular shaped block of something greenish. With considerable force, Cleea slammed it against the rock. A slender crack formed in the block. With her hands, Cleea broke off a piece and handed it to George.

He took it in his fingers tentatively, turning it over and over. "What is it?"

Cleea took a small piece for herself and placed it on her tongue. "Eat, George." She sat beside him.

George placed his piece in his dry mouth. It was salty and had a strong, vegetable flavor, like rapinni. He hated rappini. He choked. "Have you got any water in that thing?"

"Soon, George."

Soon, George. Right. Soon he'd be a dessicated corpse. Soon he'd be a snack for the vultures. What good would water do him them? Did Cleea have some kind of magic water that was going to reconstitute him? Bring him back to life once she'd achieved her apparent goal of turning him into a dessicated husk?

George chewed, urging his teeth to fight their way through the thick biscuit. It wasn't easy. He'd had jawbreakers as a kid that were easier on the jaw.

Cleea, who had apparently managed to finish off her own little piece of brick, wrapped the remaining lump back in its wrapper and returned this to her pack. She grabbed George's left hand. "How is your hand, George?"

George pulled it away. "Fine. Just fine." He pulled the amantine green slab from his mouth and tried licking the thing. It only tasted worse and so, reluctantly, he popped it back in his mouth. "Who are you, anyway?"

Cleea looked amused. Her hair possessed an unearthly, gold and red glow in the darkness. The soft sounds of the sea were lulling George back to sleep, willing him to close his eyes. Escape to another world.

"You are so funny, George." She stood. "It is good that you can keep your humor in these troubled times." She started towards the water and the dead sea creature. "Come, George. If you will assist me, we can be finished sooner."

She held out her hand and beckoned. "And drink."

That was all George needed to hear. He rose, unsteady at first, then approached Cleea who stood with her hands placed on one side of the carapace of the gigantic beached turtle. She'd done a good job of separating the shell from the body of the beast. Its carapace hung over its back now like a loose fitting hardhat.

The smell was still hideous and clumps of the animal's innards had washed up on the beach. George stepped in something jelly-like, pink and warm. "Ugh!"

He shivered and ran into the sea to wash his foot. "God, this is disgusting."

Cleea looked puzzled. "It is nothing, George. Come, assist me."

George looked at her with suspicion. "What do you want me to do?" The water was warm, like a tepid bath. He wet a finger then licked it. It was salty, though not nearly as bad as the Great Salt Lake that he'd visited a few years back with the family.

"I have loosened the shell from her body, but there is still much to do. There will be quite a lot of tissue to work against."

"Work against?" George folded his arms. Despite the warmth of the sea, a chill was seeping into his bones, heightened by the light breeze which had come sweeping in from the unseeable horizon.

"We must separate the shell. Then we will scrape it until reasonably clean."

George shivered and held back a gag reflex at the thought of 'reasonably clean.'

"Once this is done, we will align the central cartilage with the lung sacs." She raised a hand. "By morning the winds will have shifted to our advantage."

She shot George a look of supplication. "There is not much time, George."

"Right, not much time, George." George shook his head. "This is nuts. I mean, what are you doing all this for? It's not like we're going to—" George's mouth fell open. Kerplunk. A horrible thought just fell from the roof of his brain to his tongue. "You don't mean—"

George took a giant step backward. "You're not planning—" He took a another giant step and tripped over a submerged rock.

George struggled back to his feet. "You are not planning on sailing in that thing? That turtle shell?"

"Of course, George. I told you before, how else will we cross the Zephrinzee? You have another plan?"

George stammered, "What about sails?"

"I told you, the *torfu* have superior lung sacs. Quite capable of bearing the ocean wind. Have you never done this before, George?"

His head moved slowly side to side.

"How odd."

Cleea whipped her knife from under her short skirt and sliced away at the turtle's underbelly. She stuck her free hand inside and yanked out a hunk of guts. "Are you hungry, George?"

George turned pale. "Uh, no." He patted his empty stomach. "I'm still all filled up from that last little delightful green treat of yours." He rolled his eyes, figuring she'd never notice in the dark. That 'little treat' sat in his innards as comfortably as a sixteen pound shot put.

He rolled up what was left of his tattered pajama sleeves and took two giant steps forward, then a third. Once more, his choices seemed horribly limited. He could sit there at the seaside until he died—assuming he wasn't already dead—or he could pitch in, help Cleea in whatever madness she intended and see where this daft adventure led.

Summoning up all his determination, George laid his hands on the dead 'torfu', as Cleea had called it, and tugged. The wet, suctiony sound that followed turned his stomach but he fought on.

Cleea laid her hands beside his. "We must work together."

"Right." A trickle of sweat ran over George's right eye.

Twice they worked their way in a circle around the torfu, each time lifting the carapace a little further. On the third go around, they placed their feet on the bottom shell and squatted with their hands on the carapace.

"Now," said Cleea.

"I'm trying," grunted George, through gritted teeth. Side by side they attempted to rise and bring the shell up with them. Slowly, painfully the shell came free, leaking God knew what all over their feet and ankles.

The only thing George knew was that he was going to be sick. He turned his head over his shoulder and hacked up hard bits of the brick he'd eaten for dinner. Good riddance, he thought.

"Are you alright, George?"

"What?" George colored. "Yes. Something stuck in my throat."

Holding up her share of the heavy, rubbery shell with one hand, Cleea pulled out her knife once more. "Do you prefer to hold up the shell while I cut or would you do the honors?"

Honors? George's arms were shaking like a couple of slender young pine saplings in a 6.0 earthquake. How much longer could he sustain the weight of this creature's back, with or without Cleea's help? He hadn't exercised seriously since he was a kid, unless you counted his weekly golf game or the occasional bike ride with the kids.

The sharp, knife cut edges of the lower part of the shell dug into his bare feet like dull daggers. George had no idea how much his hands hurt, because he'd long ago lost all sensation in them and all they gave him now was a bit of a tingle.

He didn't know how much longer he could hang on. "You know," he said, trying to cover up the shaking in his voice that kept rhythm with the trembling in his arms and legs, "I think I would like the honors." He looked at Cleea. "If you are sure you don't mind?"

"Of course not, George."

She held her knife out by the blade. George gingerly took the handle.

"You honor Cleea and the torfu." She bowed her head.

George rolled his eyes, turning the knife in his hands. It looked dangerous. Honor the torfu? Was he insane or was she?

Cleea placed her second hand on the torfu's carapace and arched her back. "Don't worry, George. I will hold here until you are completed in your work."

Huh? George looked at the knife with uncertainty. Hell, he looked at it with mass confusion.

"Perhaps it is best if you start at the far side, cutting away the organs as you go."

"Or-organs?"

"What am I saying. Forgive me, George. You will do what is best. Take care of the lung sacs though, they are difficult to spot in the darkness as they are nearly black themselves."

Dear God, she wanted him to climb inside—inside the carcass! She was expecting him to go wading about in the dead torfu's guts!

"Hurry, George. There is not much time. The wind will be with us in the morning. Then it will turn. We do not want to be exposed on the beach past morning."

George decided not to ask why Cleea didn't want to be on the beach past morning. Though he wondered. What would they be exposed to? George had seen enough horrors already. He wasn't the least bit interested in learning what beasts might come looking for them on the beach come daylight. Best to keep some things in the unknown category.

George didn't want to be smothered in a dead turtle either. But he slowly stepped inside. He glanced over at Cleea. Her strong, muscled arms were unmoving. Could she hold the beast's back up all the while? What if her arms gave out and he was trapped inside the beast?

One thing George realized—the quicker he worked, the better his chances were of Cleea not losing her strength and him ending up smothered in torfu guts.

He counted to three under his breath and plunged into the warm, foul smelling turtle's insides. He had to bend down, in guts up to his chest, to get at the far side of the carapace.

With only a moment's hesitation, George began scraping away flesh from shell. It was hard, slow work. Stuff, long and ropy, like gristle, proved to be the hardest. He had to hack away at the stuff to break it loose. Some of the crud clinging to the inside of the shell was gooey and came right away, as easily as scooping jam.

Things got easier as he reached the center. It was high enough that he could stand here, though remaining on his feet had proven difficult. More than once he'd fallen, the first time face down, in turtle guts. After that first time, George had learned to throw his arms out the instant he felt his feet sliding out from beneath him.

"You are doing splendidly, George!" Cleea called, encouragingly.

George wiped his brow and managed a weak smile in her direction. His shoulders ached and his arms were killing him. To preserver his strength, he traded the knife back and forth from one hand to the other and back again.

Huffing, George hobbled to the opening that Cleea maintained as unbending as a Greek column. He gulped at the fresh air, a welcome respite from the fetid stench he'd been breathing for what must have been hours. "I've got to stop for a while. I need to rest."

George dropped down from the dead turtle into the water and cleaned himself off as best he could. Some of the goo had dried in his hair and clung there as tenaciously as cement. Great.

He rinsed the knife. Behind him he heard Cleea grunting. "You've done well, George."

He turned. Cleea was lifting and twisting. A godawful pile of dead turtle guts, green and brown with red sauce, sat exposed as if laid out on a plate for Christmas dinner. George was glad it was dark. As bad as that mess looked now, how would it look in the light? Now, more than ever, he agreed with Cleea's wish not to be on the beach past morning.

Who knew what sort of hungry beasties this mess might attract?

Christmas dinner. George's own thoughts came back to him. It was only a few days until Christmas, at least it had been when he'd listened to the voices, taken that little boat and jumped into the Atlantic.

Or had he missed Christmas? What time was it in this crazy world? Did they celebrate Christmas here?

George doubted it. But then, George doubted he was alive.

"I think she will come free now." Cleea shifted her hands, braced her legs and lifted some more.

George, unbidden, climbed back aboard and helped. Yet, if he was alive, he'd be in a real boat, not helping an angel build one out of a dead turtle who wanted to get to Heaven.

"Why don't you go get dressed?"

"What for?" asked Claire, looking up from her *Kids Discover* magazine.

"I don't know. But it's ten o'clock already. We just

should." Tim scooped up the empty milk container, some junk catalogs and an empty strawberry container from the little bin under the kitchen sink. It was his job to collect the recyclables and take them out to the bins in the garage. He took the bins down to the street on Fridays which was when the city recycle truck was scheduled to come by their neighborhood.

"Come on, Claire," repeated Tim as he passed behind the sofa, "get moving."

"Alright."

Tim went out to the garage, dropped the milk carton and strawberry container in the blue bin and dumped the junk mail in the yellow bin that also was used for old newspapers. He placed his hand on the door handle, set one foot on the step and froze. Something was not right. He turned. "What the—"

His father's car, the big Mercedes, was in the garage. And yet his mother had said Dad was at the office. Tim walked over to the car. The keys were still inside.

He scratched his head. This was weird. A tiny sound came from the engine area. Tim placed a hand over the hood. It was warm. The sound he'd heard had been the engine cooling.

Was Dad home? Why hadn't he said so?

Was he hiding somewhere?

–12–

George's stomach grumbled.

Cleea was up to her neck in the ocean offering up some kind of prayer to the turtle god, for all George knew, while he sat on the beach, wet, cold and hungry, hunched over, with his arms locked around himself for warmth and protection from the cool wind which had risen imperceptibly at first but now threatened to leave him hypothermic.

Incredibly, they'd fashioned a mast and sail out of body parts. Of course, the accomplishment, if accomplishment it could be considered, was all Cleea's doing. George only contributed the grunt work as needed.

Cleea held her arms out to heaven, standing there in the darkness like a sea goddess collecting her energies or communing with the universe. George didn't know which.

She came to him. "The wind is coming for us, George."

George nodded. If Cleea said the wind was coming for

them, who was he to argue?

"It's time to go, George." She held out a steely yet feminine hand.

"Go?"

"Yes, it's time to go, George."

George became befuddled. *I am not crazy I am not crazy I am not crazy.* "Are you sure—" George squinted, "—Mary?"

She nodded. "Yes, George. Who is Mary?"

I am not crazy I am not crazy I am not. He stood. Mary? Had he said Mary? Who was Mary? "Nothing. I mean, nobody."

Then he remembered, Mary was the attendant/nurse he'd had when he was. . .

He didn't want to think it through to the conclusion..

Weakly, George picked up the pack. Was he there now, he wondered, as he followed Cleea out to the water? Was Cleea Mary? Was he delusional? Had he ever gone home at all or was he still institutionalized?

George trembled. All the monsters in the world were not as frightening as this moment, could never be. He no longer knew who he was or what he was. At this very moment, he might be strapped down to a bed in a white, padded room somewhere, with Dr. Grossman and his wife staring pityingly at him through some glass window that was out of his view.

George found himself looking over his shoulder. Looking for that window.

"George?"

"Huh?" George turned. Cleea was holding the inverted carapace cum turtle ship steady. George nodded, tossed the pack aboard and hoisted himself up.

Lithely, Cleea followed suit. She quickly raised sail. George had to admit, the torfu's lung sacs were up to the task, almost as neatly as if they'd been designed for the job. They began to move and George was knocked off his feet.

"Careful, George!" shouted Cleea.

His hands clutched at the rubbery underside of the shell that now formed the unsettling deck beneath their feet. He found something cartilaginous and hard that fit into his hands like a plastic grip. He tugged. It didn't budge.

George held on. The tottering craft was picking up speed. George risked letting go, cupped his hands together and called out, "Don't you mean to ask me which way?"

Cleea turned from the sail and smiled. "I remember the way, George. Don't worry."

Famous last words, thought George. Just what Colonel Custer might have told his men. He clung to the boat while Cleea steered them out further into the dark unknown.

He watched in fascination as the beach, the high cliffs and the awful desert they'd crossed side by side blurred together and disappeared in the night. They traveled in near silence, only the occasional flapping of the sails telegraphed their passing. Slowly, George's muscles relaxed—first his neck, then his shoulders, then his legs and finally his arms. His eyelids fell and he slept.

He dreamed he was standing naked but for tattered cotton pajama bottoms on an inhospitable planetoid covered with a rocky, Mars-like desert. In the distance, a black monolith beckoned and brought a fear and dread to him all in the same instant. He wanted to run as much as he knew he needed to go forward.

And he did go forward, barefoot over the hot, rocky desert. As he approached the monolith, it became clear that this was a fortress, an ugly and imposing one, stretching from one edge of the horizon to the other.

George was sweating. George was scared to death. Yet on he marched, his feet growing bloody, his body growing weaker.

From the far left, a gray smudge quickly appeared in the impossibly high ramparts, then closed just as suddenly. A huge creature, like a giant robot monster from one of the sci-fi comic books he'd read as a child, rode out on a black chariot. Its wheels were nearly two meters high and half a meter wide. Rocks turned to dust under its tread. The robot looking creature was black, too, and carried a long whip in one massive hand.

As the creature drew closer, it was apparent that chariot and driver were one. The beast was half chariot, half robot and half something else—something powerful and cunning.

As large as it was, it managed to bear down on George in only seconds, kicking up rocks and dust in the thin, alien air.

George coughed, his lungs filling with sand. He spat and stood his ground. The big arm drew back over the monster's right shoulder. The black whip swung back like a headless snake, twisting and coiling in the throes of death. The arm snapped forward and the black whip, thick as George's forearm, lashed out at him like a hot, giant blue-black tongue.

The tip of the whip bit into his flesh, scalding his skin and tearing open his belly.

Hi-el. The word imposed itself into George's brain. *Hi-el. Remember me, George. Hiel. Fear me, George.*

George woke, shaking and wet. He screamed and clutched his belly.

Cleea, holding onto the tip of the sail, balanced on her haunches, looked at him, thoughtfully. "You dream, George?"

He nodded. A tiny shiver swept over him like a mini-quake.

"You should eat." She fastened the end of the sail with something reminiscent of turtle guts. "And drink."

With her knife, she carefully opened a hole in one of two bulging greenish-white sacs or organs attached to the shell. Cleea had reminded George not to remove these. He wondered now what she had in mind for them.

Having cut an opening the size of a softball, she pushed her hand into the first of the two things and withdrew a wet, greenish mass. She pushed the oozy mess towards George.

"Yes?"

"Take it."

"Why?" George cringed away. The stuff reeked.

"Food."

"No, thanks," replied George. "That can't possibly be food. Besides, I'm a vegetarian."

"It's not animal, George."

"It's not?"

"The torfu carries digested seaweed, kelp, algae and plankton in this sac. The energy reserves support the torfus in great crossings or times of scarcity."

As much as George wanted to puke, he stuck his finger into the mush. It was cold and wet and smelled like a poorly filtered aquarium. Before he could protest, Cleea had thrust the rest of the stuff into his hands.

After watching Cleea repeat the procedure for herself and seeing her down a handful of the gook in half a dozen bites, George put his tongue to the green goop. It tasted mostly like salt.

He ate. Trying really hard not to think about what it was and most of all where it had come from. "Hey, this isn't bad," he said, chewing and growing accustomed to the taste and the oddly spongy texture.

"I'm glad you are happy, George." Cleea smiled and rinsed her hands in the sea, wiped them on her skirt.

Happy? thought George. Happy was not the word on his lips—his sore chapped lips.

Was he happy? Sitting in a scooped out turtle shell in the middle of an unknown ocean in an unknown land, eating the poor dead turtle's secondhand green dinner? This was one dream he wasn't about to share with Elaine.

A tiny bubble crossed between his eyes and landed on his nose. Was it his imagination? Where did that come from? He chuckled and swatted it away.

Cleea was back at the helm.

Another bubble landed on his arm. It was transparent and glassy with a trace of pink inside. George poked it with a finger. Pop! It disappeared.

Maybe it would work on him as well. He poked himself in the belly, half-expecting to pop. But he didn't. George tried again, pressing his finger deep into his flesh.

Nothing.

Another bubble bounced off his cheek. This one was larger, about the size of a ping pong ball. It burst and stung George's eyes. "Oww!"

"What is wrong?" Cleea asked.

"Nothing," said George. "Just some goofy bubbles." He waved his arms in front of his face, fighting off a nearing trio, each bubble the size of a tennis ball.

Cleea gasped.

"What?" George asked. "What's wrong? They're only bubbles."

Cleea ran to her pack, removed her light and held it high above her head. "Look, George. They come."

"They?"

"More bubbles."

George stood, leaning against the makeshift mast, trying hard to see nearly invisible bubbles in the dark. It was about as easy as looking for eight balls in the La Brea Tar Pits.

"Over there, port side!"

George followed the line of Cleea's arm. A pinkish haze grew in the distance. Bubbles, big ones, a meter or more in diameter, were bouncing along the surface heading towards them.

"They're coming this way," said George. "What are they? Why are you worried about them? They're only bubbles. Annoying I agree," he said, rubbing his still stinging eyes, "but hardly dangerous."

Cleea was shaking her head in obvious disagreement. "They come for us, George. He sends them." Her nostrils tested the air. "Chlorine gas."

"What?" George stepped back, knocking into Cleea. "Sorry. What do you mean 'he sends them'? Are you telling me somebody is sending us chlorine gas?"

Cleea nodded. The bubbles were growing larger now. She dodged to avoid one the size of her head. Several smaller ones bounced off their arms and legs.

One caught in George's throat. He coughed. His nostrils burned and he was finding it hard to breathe. Glassy bubbles the size of basketballs bounced over the boat. George ducked and threw his hands over his face.

When he looked up, Cleea was fighting to brace the sails side to side. George got the idea. They could erect a wall. The bubbles would bounce right off and away.

He scrambled to his feet. "Let me help!"

Cleea nodded. "Quickly, George!" She pointed. The bubbles were huge now, as tall as the mast and no more than thirty meters off.

George grabbed the bottom of the sail on the right. There was no way to hold it against the wind and the bubbles. He had to attach it somehow. If not, they could wrap themselves inside, using the sails like blankets. That might protect them from the gas.

Might.

He tugged the sail, stretching it far to the side. It barely reached. A little more and he could affix it to a crack in the shell. Cleea was still fighting to attach her side of the sails. She was breathing hard. Bubbles burst all around her. She fell to her knees.

"Just need a little more," muttered George, through clenched teeth. Holding the sail's edge, he pulled himself up onto the narrow lip of the shell. Behind him, the black sea was churning. Gigantic bubbles of deadly gas bounced in his direction. The first one caught the wind and leapt right over his head, but the next one was skirting along the water's surface, heading straight for him.

Cleea was on her knees, coughing, attempting to hold out the sail on the other side, but the chlorine gas was overwhelming her.

Panicky, watching as his own death approached swiftly and silently, George yanked on the sail with all his might. "Whoa!" The boat rocked and sea spray raked his back. He'd nearly lost his grip. He tugged again.

For a moment, nothing happened. Then he heard a tear. The lower part of the sail had come loose from the mast. "Damn!" In frustration, George pulled again. The boat tipped awkwardly in his direction. Cleea was sliding towards him. Fearfully, George let go.

The boat rocked violently and he flew overboard.

"George!" shouted Cleea.

George felt the water cover his head, fill his ears. He kicked out with his arms and legs. The sounds of a violent crash vibrated through the water as George fought his way up.

Gasping he reached what should have been the surface but it was preternaturally dark. He coughed and the sound reverberated. His head struck something soft and rubbery. He reached out with one hand.

He was trapped beneath the torfu's shell! He wanted to scream but barely had the breath for living let alone a good healthy scream.

Blindly, he kicked out and after several moments of thrashing struck something hard, long and round. The mast. Trembling, George held on.

Where was Cleea?

"Cleea?" George coughed as he caught a mouthful of warm seawater. "Cleea?" Nothing but the echo of the waves and his own frightened voice.

George dove. The water was impossibly dark and stung his eyes. He rose to the surface, caught his breath and dove again, staying near the mast at first, afraid of losing his orientation.

Something grabbed his arm. His mouth opened reflexively and instantly George regretted it, receiving a mouthful of brackish water for his rashness.

It was Cleea. She had the light necklace around her neck. Her pack was tangled in the sail. She pointed behind her.

George nodded.

Swimming around behind her, he found the tip of the sail had wrapped itself around her backpack. He pulled. No way. He needed Cleea's knife.

He gestured to Cleea and she pulled out her knife. George took it and quickly cut away the sail. Feeling like he was going to burst—George had never held his breath this long in all his life—George and Cleea clung to one another and hurried upward.

Breaking the surface, George rasped, taking in a grateful breath of fresh air. George clung to the broken mast with one arm. Cleea lifted the light over her head and hung it over a tiny outcropping on the mast. Her fingers reached out, tightly gripping George's shoulder. "Thank you, George."

"Thank you?"

"You saved us."

Wheezing, George looked at Cleea, dumbstruck. "Saved us? I almost got us killed!"

Cleea wiped wet hair from her eyes. "The chlorine gas almost killed us, George. Your quick thinking saved us." Cleea gazed overhead. "Even now, the deadly gas passes above. We are safe here. The air is pure." She squeezed. "Thank you, George."

George coughed, holding onto the crooked mast with one hand and wiping away the spittle that ran down his stubbly chin with the other. There was a lingering scent of chlorine in the air, as if they were in a giant, underground swimming pool.

If that was the case, he hoped some kind soul would toss him a clean, dry towel and point him in the direction of the chaise lounges and fetch him one of those cool, colorful, tropical drinks with the paper umbrellas floating in them.

"I think we should stay here for a while longer," Cleea said. She turned off the light and placed it back over her neck. "There is no point wasting energy."

"Sure," said George. Like they had any choice. Did Cleea believe they could right their homemade boat?

They hung on in silence, but for the echoing splashes of water trapped beneath the shell with them. Time, if there was such a thing, passed like a long, dark, blank screen. George was exhausted and fought to stay alert. He was frightened he'd fall asleep once more, let go of the mast and quietly drown.

George felt something small pass quickly between his legs—most likely a fish of some sort—and said, "I hope there are no sharks out here."

"Sharks? Oh, I don't think we need to worry, George. The flesh eaters are attracted by blood. . ." she paused, then added, "or fear."

Oh great, thought George, thinking of his poor lacerated body. And if he was scared before, he was terrified now. Cleea's words echoed unanswered under the carapace.

George tried vainly to think of something different, something light, cheerful and agreeable.

Something that wouldn't make him shark bait.

But a traitorous little corner of his brain would not let

him. George didn't like tight spaces and George didn't like dark, confined spaces much better.

He was trapped and he was sure the air was getting stale, losing oxygen, filling with deadly carbon dioxide. He was going to die. How would he explain that to his wife and kids? That he'd died floating around under a giant turtle shell while avoiding equally giant bubbles of chlorine gas.

Would he see them in Heaven? Would Elaine, Tim and Claire be waiting for him as he fought his way through Hell?

Letting go of the mast and following the sweeping arc of the inverted shell with his hands, George made his way to the outer edge. "I'm going to see what's happening out there."

"Be careful, George. There may be dangers."

George held back a response. How could he admit that he was afraid to remain in the dark? Trapped like a bug in a jar.

He took a deep breath and went under, careful to keep his hands on the shell, fearful that he would lose his grasp and be left drifting alone in that unknown sea.

He lifted his head up quickly on the other side. Mindful of the sting of the chlorine, he took a sniff before opening his eyes. The air seemed okay.

He cracked open an eye. It was dark but not as dark as before. It was quiet, too. He hauled himself up the rubbery, wet carapace on his stomach. It was like holding onto a dense foam pool mattress. The wind was pushing them along like a floating island. The horizon was featureless and dark gray.

George slid back down and told Cleea what he'd seen.

"That is good," replied Cleea. "All goes well. Come,

George." She dove under the surface and disappeared.

All goes well? George felt like screaming. So far he'd been nearly eaten by a cave monster with banana breath, trapped in a hole, buried alive to save himself from a giant bird that would have given a pterydactyl a run for his money, and almost bowled over by giant bubbles filled with deadly chlorine gas while floating along the ocean on a scraped out turtle shell!

This was 'going well'?

"Cleea?" George's fists struck the surface. "Damn! She's gone!" George dived under the water and came out on the other side. The angel was making her way up the torfu's shell using her knife like a piton, driving it in handhold after handhold, a good thirty centimeters at a time.

She stretched out on her belly atop the flattish center of the 'boat' and held out her hand. "Come, George."

George wheezed and shook his head, sending showers through the air. Did she really think he was going to climb that thing? It'd be one step forward and two steps back. No, he'd never make it. "The knife. Toss me down the knife." Though he had little faith his muscles could carry him up as easily as Cleea had managed.

"No need, George. Place your hands and feet in the gouges I made coming up."

George looked at the surface of the shell. He stuck his hand in the lowest of the knife wounds. It fit and provided him some purchase. Cleea was right. This wasn't so hard after all.

Just disgusting.

George braced himself and climbed quickly. Too quickly. On the third step, he slipped and landed on his back in the water. The boat was drifting away. Thrashing his arms and kicking his legs as fast as he could, he managed to close the distance.

George grabbed onto the shell, worked his way around to the side. This time he climbed more carefully. Cleea assisted him as he came within reach of her grasp.

They sat side by side, facing what looked to be the dawn. There was no way they could control their rate of speed or their destination.

"Any idea where we are?" he said at last. They'd drifted into an endless patch of seaweed as golden as sargassum. George feared they'd get stuck in the thick stuff.

"We are here, George."

She'd said it with such sincerity that George couldn't even get angry with her. Of course, they were here. How stupid of him not to notice.

A dark band grew on the distant horizon, pencil thin at first, but growing taller. The seaweed was thinning out. George prayed it was land ahead and not the edge of the world that they were soon going to go sailing over.

"We'll arrive soon," Cleea said, folding her knees up to her chin and wrapping her arms around them. She closed her eyes.

George kept his open—looking for killer bubbles. . .and monsters. For it seemed no matter where you went, the world was filled with monsters. And that included this world.

—13—

Of all the things in the world, it reminded George of the coast of southern California, somewhere up around Santa Barbara, the way it might have looked a couple of hundred years ago. The sky was bluer here. The hills were brown and green. Some rose to sharp, craggy heights, others were more soft in form and tree covered.

The beach they were approaching was wide and broad with yellow sand. A natural harbor cut into the continent—if continent it was—to their right. George could make out a long wharf and scores of piers appearing and disappearing in the lifting fog.

But that wasn't surprising. After all, there was an entire town spread among the rolling hills, looking as if it had comfortably lain there for ages. Smoke, gray and black, rose sluggishly from distant chimneys. The place was huge. There had to be thousands of buildings here, though none stood taller than three stories.

George rubbed dried sea salt from his stubbled chin. "What is this place?"

"This is Ryaii, George," answered Cleea. "Has it changed so much that you no longer recognize her?"

Before he could raise a reply, she said, "The waves have stopped pushing us. We are stalled." Cleea checked to see that her pack was secure, stood, brought her legs together, lifted her arms over her head and dived.

She resurfaced and called to him. "Come, George." Cleea lowered her head and began swimming towards the shoreline.

"Oh, sure," George mumbled, struggling, his feet aching. "It's only a couple hundred meters. No problem."

He looked from his toes to the beach, attempting to get some measure of just how far he might be able to dog-paddle before sinking to the bottom. Halfway?

There was only one way to find out.

George hit the water with about as much grace as a seal—a seal who'd been heavily tranquilized and tossed over on its stomach. The water was surprisingly cooler here. Much cooler than it had been on the opposite shore. He stretched his aching arms and began swimming. He'd never felt so stiff and so sore in all his life. How could he be dead if he felt so much pain?

Cleea was a couple dozen strokes ahead of him. George swam on. His breath grew labored. The tide was against him. He only hoped there weren't any riptides. He slipped under and came up coughing.

Cleea turned back and called out to him. "We're nearly there, George."

George, mindful of keeping his mouth shut and determined to breathe through his nose, nodded and pushed on. His legs were growing heavy, and about as useful as a couple of rolled up, waterlogged Sunday newspapers.

While he dog-paddled the last forty yards or so, Cleea rose from the waves as effortlessly as a sea goddess, shook her head and rested on her haunches while she waited for George to beach himself. And beach himself he did, like a lost and confused baby sperm whale. He didn't so much come to shore as the shore came up and hit him.

On hands and knees, he pushed himself slowly, breathlessly up past the water's edge.

Cleea offered her hand. "We have done well, George." She pulled him to his unsteady feet. "It is good to be home, yet there is much to do. Come, George."

She turned on her heels and headed towards the street which ran parallel to the beach. It was a good ten meters above the shoreline and the ground there was braced with a broad wooden wall that looked like it could stand up to a typhoon.

George nodded, rasped incoherently, took one step and had almost managed another, when he collapsed in on himself like a punctured blow-up doll.

"Hi, Mom."

"Timmy, Claire! What are you doing here?"

Tim thought his mother looked more scared than surprised. "We thought we'd come by the office."

"How did you get here?"

"Dad's car."

"Tim, you really should have called first before taking the car like that."

"Sorry."

"We thought we could all have lunch together," added Claire. "I want to go to Taco Bell."

"Lunch?" Mrs. Richards looked worriedly at her children.

"Yeah, are you okay, Mom?" Tim leaned his head around the cubicle where his dad hid out. It was empty and his dad's computer wasn't even switched on. "Where's Dad?"

"Your father had a meeting." Mrs. Richards rose and picked up her purse. "You know, I think lunch is a good idea: I'll just tell the girls we're going and to answer the phones."

Tim blocked the doorway. "What kind of a meeting?"

"Meeting?"

"Yeah, you said Dad was in a meeting. What kind, Mom?"

"Oh, uh, well." Mrs. Richards was fishing around in her purse for the keys to the Volvo. "I think he went to see a man about a boat." She smiled, pushed Tim's arm out of the way and headed for the door.

"Hooray!" shouted Claire. "I hope we're getting that cabin cruiser that I liked best, don't you, Tim?"

"Yeah, sure, Claire," he replied. Mom was lying to them. Tim was certain of it. The question remained: why was she lying to them? And where was their dad?

He dreamed he was standing naked again, but for tattered cotton pajama bottoms on an inhospitable planetoid covered with a rocky, Mars-like desert. His stomach, slashed from groin to sternum, oozed pus and blood. The skin lifted away from his sides as if inviting Death.

Not far ahead, the black monolith beckoned once more and brought back memories—were they dreams or were they real—of fear and dread. George wanted to run and knew that he could not.

He went forward, the smell of his burning bare feet bringing waves of nausea as he crossed the rocky, lifeless desert one painful step after another.

The monolith loomed above him, as dark and imposing as ever. Filling the horizon like a sea of evil. And he knew what would happen next.

And it did.

George's trembling body flashed from hot to cold and back again, leaving a trail of blood in his wake.

From the near left, a gray smudge quickly appeared in the impossibly high ramparts, then closed just as suddenly. The huge creature, who wielded his long, black whip, like a knife, had returned.

The huge black chariot turned sharply in his direction and came straight for him. All the more frightening as it made no sound as it tore up the ground and crushed the black rocks beneath its wheels as it came.

The creature drew closer. Again, George knew what would happen next.

And again it did.

Coming to a halt some twenty meters distant, a cloud of gray dust obscuring its massive wheels, with something resembling a grin on its mad, cunning face, the monster studied him with obvious disdain. The big arm drew back once more over the creature's shoulder.

George choked, his lungs filling with sand. He stood his ground, unable to do more. For the second time, the black whip swung back like a headless snake twisting and coiling in the throes of death. The creature's arm snapped forward, as George knew it would. He braced himself on the bloody stumps of his feet. His hands feebly spread out across the open wound over his torso as if they had some impossible chance of warding off the coming blow.

The black whip, thick as George's forearm, lashed out at him with its hot, giant blue-black tongue.

George flinched. The tip of the whip chewed into his shoulder and licked his neck. He screamed.

Hi-el. The words imposed themselves into George's brain as deeply as if they'd been burned into his corpus callosum with a branding iron. *Hi-el. Do not forget, George. Hiel. Fear me, George. Go back or face your doom.*

A rush of bitterness swept over George's tongue and burned its way down his throat. He felt as if he was chewing on a handful of dry aspirins.

He screamed and opened his eyes. The world was a pool of grayness dancing before his blind eyes.

Something grabbed his quaking hand. He squeezed.

"George!"

A towel was lifted from George's eyes and the grayness disappeared. He was lying on some sort of bed. The dark shape nearby held his hand.

They were in a small, hexagonal room with a low roof. A dull glow coming from the opposite wall provided the only light. "Cleea?" His taste buds still fought that unsavory memory. Was it part of his dream? And was that dream all part of this other dream?

Oh god, he thought. I really am going crazy.

"No, George. I am Sharan."

"Where-where's Cleea?" George tipped his head up and felt a burning sensation rip through his neck like a giant pair of wire cutters.

The woman or angel, or whatever she was, pushed George gently down. "Careful, George. You must rest. Cleea will return soon. She meets with the others. She will return soon. Until then, you are in my charge."

She adjusted the thin sheet that covered his body. "I will bring you some food and drink." She paused, framed in the doorway. "Have you a preference?"

"Sure," said George, his body a knot of agony, as if he were buried up to his eyebrows in a colony of red ants, the sun beating down, his brain turning into a lather of madness, "bring me a glass of hemlock and an Effexor sandwich."

"George?"

George chuckled and his ribs threatened to buckle. "Never mind. Whatever you bring will be perfect."

The form disappeared.

George was alone with his silence. A word, small as a speck of dust drifting through space, floated through the air, growing larger as it slowly fell into George's mind.

Hi-el. Hi-el.

George trembled. But then, the sheet was thin and he was cold. Wasn't he?

It was Christmas morning. Claire and Tim were opening their colorful packages. Glittering reds and greens, billowy oversized purple ribbons. The tree gave off a nearly delicious scent of pine. George smelled coffee brewing in the kitchen. This was the best Christmas ever.

He'd even bought Elaine those new topaz earrings in the platinum settings she'd been hinting about for months. Claire got a big bottle of ketchup from Santa Claus. The crazy kid asked for one every year. George loved her for it.

Tim looked happiest with his new trumpet. George begged him to play something Christmasy on it. Tim obliged by performing a solo interpretation of Jingle Bells.

"Terrific!" George clapped in deep admiration. Both his kids were wonderful and gifted.

Elaine and the kids had gotten George a new putter, some golf balls with his initials on them and a humongous book about boats. It was so heavy, he could barely lift it. "Geez," he said with delight, "we won't need to buy a boat—just put a mast and some sails on this thing."

While Claire was busy fussing with her new doll, George helped himself to one of the chocolates that had spilled out of her Christmas stocking.

Yep, it was the best Christmas ever.

Elaine sat down beside him, on the arm of the leather sofa. She placed her hand on his neck and rubbed. "Are you happy, George?"

"Huh? Sure. Happy." George patted his wife's leg. Happy. Was he happy? Mentally, he shrugged. He was as happy as he could be given the circumstances. Christmas was better than most. If only happiness could come more often than Christmas.

That would be something, wouldn't it? The children tore open their remaining packages. The smiles on their faces were impossible to erase.

"Come, George." She pulled his hand.

"What?" The kids were fading. The Christmas tree lights flickered, then blurred.

"I have something for you."

"What?"

"George?"

The room came back into focus. It was that angel again. What was her name? Sharan. She was a head shorter than Cleea but every bit as athletically built. Her long straight hair was of blackest ebony, though it seemed to sparkle with diamond dust. Where had Elaine gone? What had happened to the children, Tim and Claire?

Sharan placed a tray on the table beside the bed. "I have something for you."

George looked at her in confusion.

"Your food."

He looked at the tray. Some items resembling bread and fruit lay before him. George picked up something thick-skinned and orange-hued. He held it to his nose. It smelled like pineapple. In the center of the tray was a glazed clay pitcher.

Sharan caught him looking at it. "It is water."

Water. What do you know? George was beginning to think these creatures drank no more than camels.

She turned to the far wall and extended her hands. The wall shimmered. The room grew brighter.

Nice trick, thought George.

Sharan turned back to him. "It is no trick, George."

George's heart leapt to his throat and he nearly choked on the red, clotted muscle. Dear God, these creatures could read his mind!

But then, he should have known. They were angels, after all.

Suddenly, his heart sank into his chest like a heavy stone. He thought again of Elaine, Tim and Claire. Were they real? Were they simply part of some ongoing dream of his? Reality was growing harder and harder to discern. How would he know when he had worked his way back to sanity? How would he determine that he'd finally gone completely mad?

George shook his head and tugged at the thin sheet that covered him as if it were a shred of reality.

"If you have no further needs, I will leave you now. Nourish yourself, George."

George nodded. Real or not, he missed his family.

He needed to move. He needed to get moving. Not stay in one place. Ignoring the food, George rose. The floor was dull gray stone. His feet were bare. He was naked. Looking about the room, whose walls themselves appeared to be the same hard, gray stone as the floor, he found a pair of simple, pocketless and zipperless, tan trousers. He pulled them up to his waist and adjusted the drawstring.

"Not bad." He rubbed his stomach. Was it his imagination or had he lost weight? He pinched his love handles. All that marching and the lack of food had done at least one good thing for him. He'd lost a few unnecessary pounds. Elaine would be glad about that. An equally simplistic, long-sleeved, brown shirt, that had the feel and texture of stiff cotton, completed his outfit.

George didn't see any shoes so he went barefoot. He came out on a narrow undulating, flagstone street. Cottages, similar to the one he'd left, or possibly escaped from, pushed up to the edges of the road as if trying to squeeze it out of existence. The stones nearest the edges seemed to buckle under the challenge. A sweet and pungent odor filled the air.

A chunky-faced man in a dark tunic came down the road, nodded in George's direction and plodded silently on. George followed.

The man turned sharply at the bottom of the hill and continued on. George's bare feet thudded against the cold stones as he pursued. Why he was following the man, he did not know. Where would it lead him?

The man turned off onto a road so narrow in breadth that the folks living there could very probably have reached out their front windows to shake hands with one another. George passed few other souls, somberly dressed and pale faced strangers, and an inexplicable obsession with the chunky-faced man drove him along.

The man rapped on a rough-hewn wooden door, then pulled on the handle to enter without waiting for a reply from within.

George paused in the street. His breath came out in a fog. The stranger had entered a squat, thick stone building whose walls were ash gray. In the front window, the only window, were unusual trinkets, pieces of metal in unrecognizable shapes serving unknown purposes.

George pressed his face against the glass. A pleated, dust-covered black curtain prevented his gaze from penetrating further. The sign jutting out from the door had been formed of metal bits and pieces as well. George had to squint, then step back, before the name became clear. *Apotheosis.*

How odd, thought George. What sort of place was this? He looked up and down the empty street. Where was everybody?

George placed his fingers through the handle and pulled. The door protested, fighting to hold to the doorframe, then gave with a creak of despair. Taking a last look down the street, George ducked inside.

Rough, uncaring hands grabbed him and pushed him against a dark wall. A thick wool blanket, smelling like it had last done duty wiping dry a damp alpaca, fell over his head. He fought as the blanket was squeezed tightly around his body, forcing his arms to his sides.

George's feet left the ground and he felt himself being hoisted up over someone's back. "Hey, what do you think you're doing? Who are you?" George twisted to no avail. "Let go of me!"

"Quiet," grumbled his captor.

"Yeah, keep it shut," came a second voice. "Hold him still while I tie off this rope, man."

George felt a rope being wrapped around his body and soon he was bound as tightly as a mummy in a sightless sarcophagus.

George heard shuffling feet coming from yet another source. So, there were three of them at least. Maybe more. But what on earth did they want with him? Were they kidnaping him or set on murdering him? "Won't you at least—"

A painful crack on the skull was the last thing George remembered before slowly coming to his senses. He was still being carried and from the way his body was being jostled, it was apparent that he was being hauled down a steep stairway. His feet bounced recklessly off the walls.

His captor was silent but for the force of his breathing.

After a time, the footsteps leveled off and the sound of the other man's shoes echoed loudly.

"Toss him over there."

"Right."

George braced himself. Whoever had been bearing him lifted him easily as a sofa cushion and tossed him into the air. George gasped and braced himself. Half a second later, he landed in something rough but yielding and fought to get back the wind that had been knocked out of him.

"Comfortable, George?" came a sadistic voice out of the darkness.

"Shut up, fool. You want him to recognize you?" another voice whispered harshly.

"Aww." The man lashed out and kicked George in the side.

George felt his ribs give.

"Don't move," ordered the man with the high, squealy voice.

George held completely still. After a time, he heard nothing. Had they gone? He worked his tingling arms side to side. Could he escape?

He moved his legs, waiting to see if this elicited any response from his captors. None came. No threats. No more vicious kicks.

Working deliberately, George managed to slowly work his way down and out of the hot and suffocating blanket until he was far enough out to get his hands free from within. Pulling at the thick rope and blanket together, he managed to extract his head.

He threw his bonds aside and gulped in cool, dank air. Taking in his surroundings for the first time, George saw that he was lying atop a pile of coarse burlap sacks. From the scent and texture, they might have been filled with coffee beans.

He stood. The stone-walled room was tight and low-ceilinged. The only light cut like a king-sized arrowhead beneath the terribly sturdy looking door at the far end which was six steps up off the floor.

He was alone and he was trapped.

—14—

George banged his fists against the cold, uncaring walls. The floor and walls were solid, impenetrable and inescapable. Would those men leave him to die here?

His jail cell was as frigid as a walk-in refrigerator. He tried the door. Locked, like he knew it would be. Must be. The hardware was steel. He'd need the key to get out that way.

Crawling on his hands and knees, George scoured the room for another exit. He pried into the corners until his fingers bled. Yet it was to no avail.

The smell of whatever was in the sacks made him recognize his gnawing hunger. He loosened the string that held a bag shut and looked inside. He ran his hands through dark, brown beans.

George raised a handful to his nose. It was coffee, no doubt, though it carried a sweetish scent, sweeter than any coffee he'd ever smelled. He put a bean on his tongue and bit into it.

He spat. Not good. But it gave him another idea. Whether it had a chance of working would depend on his captors returning and when; and their intelligence or lack thereof.

George hurried.

Opening a number of the sacks, George transferred handfuls of coffee beans from a sack he had chosen in the center of the pile. When this central sack had been reduced to half full, George retied the remaining bags and put everything back in order.

He left the half empty sack in the middle unsealed. That sack was for him. He lowered himself into the bag and pulled beans up and over his neck, shoulders, and face as best he could. He pulled the bag shut from the inside.

Everything depended on his captors believing he had escaped. But would they? Or would they simply search the coffee sacks until he was discovered?'

That gave George another idea. Listening first to be sure the coast was clear, he rose from the sack and tiptoed to the door. He ripped a tiny scrap of cloth from his new trousers, pulling hard at the cuff of the left leg until a slender strip of material tore free. He stuck it under the crack between the door and the stone floor, rubbing it against the jagged bottom edge of the door until it stuck to the wood on the far side.

He hoped that would be enough to make it look as though he caught his trousers on the door on his way out.

"Maybe that will get there attention," whispered George.

He hurried back to his hiding place and waited.

His wait was a long one. His bent figure grew stiff and tired. Time after time, he shifted his weight. As he did so, the beans made loud scrunching noises that he feared would arouse his jailers.

He marked his time by trying to separate what he thought was reality from what appeared to be reality. In dreams, he could often will them to go in one direction or another. Like a pleasant erotic dream. He tried willing himself back home, in his bed, dreaming about boats and the ocean. Instead of lying in a mound of sickly sweet coffee beans, imagine yourself lying in bed.

No. That could be a hospital bed. And he did not want to be back there. Imagine yourself in a boat in the ocean. Claire and Tim are there, all smiles. Elaine is fixing a boater's lunch in the galley below.

He could still smell the coffee beans. He could feel them, all around him, insinuating themselves into his hair, under his skin, their odor filling his nose. This was one tough dream. George longed to move but feared he could not control the dream that he was locked in.

What had become of Cleea? Who were these men? What did they plan for him when they returned?

George twisted and rubbed his throbbing neck. Maybe they were never coming back. Maybe he should look for another avenue of escape?

The sound of approaching steps brought these thoughts of George's to a complete halt. He made himself even smaller and held his breath.

"Hey, what's this?"

"What?"

"This!" shouted the squeaky voiced man.

"It's a bit of cloth. So what?"

"So what? That's what he was wearing is so what."

"Are you certain, Olaf?"

"I hauled him down here, didn't I? The bottoms of his legs were sticking out in my face. I know what I saw."

"Well, open it up and be quick, then!"

Every nerve in George's body came to red alert as the key turned in the lock and the door swung open with a low moan.

"Is he there?"

"I don't know. Stop jabbering and look about."

"Bring a light."

There followed the sound of running footsteps.

"He's not here!" shouted Squeaky.

"He's got to be! It will be our skins if he's not. Search the sacks. Maybe he's hiding."

"Yeah, you're right."

This was the moment of truth. George heard the big bags of coffee beans being tossed about. Suddenly, he felt himself being lifted into the air. Praying all the while, George held the top of the bag shut with his hands. If it fell open, all was lost. A moment later he was flying through the air blindly.

The sack hit the wall, crushing George's shoulder on impact. He bit his tongue and tasted blood as he fell to the ground, landing on his side. Fighting to remain still and keep his breath under control he waited for the big man to uncover him.

"He isn't here," Squeaky said. "How did he get out is what I want to know."

"He's tricked us. I knew it was not going to be so simple. He's too crafty for that."

"Where could he be?"

"I don't know," said the second fellow, with the voice George remembered as being the one belonging to the fellow who'd tied him up earlier. "We'd better search every room. We can't have him wandering around."

George heard both pairs of footsteps hurrying up the stairs. He closed his eyes and prayed. Everything depended on what he did or didn't hear next.

The footsteps faded into nothing. George smiled. He had not heard the sound of the heavy door being closed. Slowly, he relaxed his grip on the sack's opening and stuck his head through. A welcome ball of light greeted his eyes.

He was free.

Beep-beep. That was the sound the computer made when a dictation was completed. Elaine lifted her foot from the pedal. The report was finished? She didn't even remember transcribing it. She looked at the computer screen. Bits and pieces. A word here, a phrase there. Some of it, most of it, made no sense at all. That part in the middle—*I am not crazy*—had she really typed that?

Frustrated and annoyed with herself, she pushed her toe down hard on the left part of the pedal, sending the recording back to the beginning. She'd have to start again. She rubbed her face and yawned.

Elaine checked her logbook while she waited for her report to return to its beginning. She wasn't getting a damn thing done today at all. For the umpteenth time, she caught herself looking across the room to the little corner where George liked to hide. He wasn't there. Where was George hiding now?

–15–

George crept to the steps.

Sounds of confusion and commotion echoed through the doorway. He took the tall sharp chiseled steps slowly, clinging to the side of the wall as he went. The door opened onto a small antechamber. There was a glowing orb attached to the ceiling. So, that was the source of the light.

Three dark passages led away from the antechamber, like spokes on a parlous wheel. Sounds came from the central passage. That left two likely choices, the left and the right. Too bad Cleea wasn't here, thought George, she'd simply ask me which way to go and I'd pick one.

"Over here."

George jumped at the plaintive whisper. A broad, coarse-haired, dark-skinned man dressed in breechcloth appeared in the tunnel on the right. He wore black, military style boots. His short, yet powerful-looking forearm beckoned.

George looked at the man with eyes of distrust. Forearms like that could kill him, pluck him apart like a roasted goose.

The stranger stepped further into the light. His gnarly nostrils flared. "Quickly. They come back."

That much of what the fierce looking man said was true. George could hear the sounds of footsteps returning down the central passage. He nodded.

"Follow me." The stranger waved George on and stepped back into the shadowy corridor.

Off they went down a series of passages that cut right and left without reason. Fear hung in George's throat. If he lost sight of the man in front of him, he'd be doomed for certain. He had no idea where he was. Escape would be nearly impossible. Recapture by the men who'd kidnapped him would be inevitable.

George's potential savior stopped before a well-lit hall. On the high walls were paintings, images of death and despair, the works of a solitary and suffering madman.

The stranger whispered, "Take heed." His pale blue eyes locked onto George's and held them as if it were an atomic bond.

George nodded. He'd been taking heed since this entire nightmare had begun.

There were three doors along each side of the hall. The stranger crept to the middle door on the left and pressed his ear to the well-oiled wood. He nodded to George and motioned for him to come. He held a finger to his lips, warning George to keep silent.

George tiptoed to the door. The stranger twisted the handle and said in sotto voce, "It is unlocked. I believe the room to be empty. Thudor and the others seek you. They believe you are far from here."

"Yes?" George felt there was more coming; something that the stranger left unsaid.

"If anyone is here, we must subdue them. Ready?"

Subdue them? What did this nut expect him to do? Before George could answer, the stranger had thrown open the door and leapt inside. Without thinking, perhaps not wanting to be left alone in the great hall, George followed.

One man, or rather some Earthbound giant from another world, gray skinned, with a head as large as a basketball, sat at a long, wooden table. He was leaning back in his seat, with his arms folded over his chest and his feet propped up on the tabletop. He opened his lugubrious eyes with a start.

George's companion leapt through the air in a blur and was on the giant before he could raise himself. The stranger's right arm locked around the giant's neck and squeezed. The giant struggled to his feet, kicking the chair away. The chair struck the wall and collapsed in splinters.

George stood frozen, not knowing what to do or even which side in the affair to take. The giant was rocking side to side, his face turning white as he fought to remove the smaller man's death hold on his neck.

In a mad dash, the giant ran to the nearest wall, slamming the smaller man's back against the stone. George expected his companion to collapse in a pile of broken bones and bleeding arteries, yet he hung on like a bulldog. A rictus of pain arced across his face. He appeared to squeeze his foe all the harder.

The giant tottered, scratching at his attacker's arms until they bled. As suddenly as it had begun, it was over. The giant coughed and fell.

The stranger lay across the dead giant, breathing hard. After a moment he rose and looked in George's direction. Until that instant, George hadn't realized the surge of adrenalin rushing through every inch of his body. Fear and apprehension gripped him. Was he to be next?

The stranger was panting. "We'll need weapons." He jumped up from his victim and ran to the far wall.

Only then did George take in the rest of the room. The room was low-ceilinged and appeared to be an armory. Weapons of every sort—knives, battle axes, broadswords and more hung on three of the four walls.

The stranger picked a nasty looking blade a meter long and tested it in the air. He moved the sword in a flash of speed George would not have thought possible. The sharp tip flashed like a shooting star.

The man nodded, satisfied. "What would you choose?"

"Me?" George looked at the man as if he'd lost his mind. "You can't be serious. I don't know how to use one of those things."

The stranger eyed him skeptically.

"Oh, all right," said George. Anything to get moving. The place smelled of death.

George went to the wall and examined the deadly looking

instruments. The swords were long and heavy. One look at the maces told him that if he tried to wield one of the murderous things he'd only end up killing himself— with a short, embarrassing blow to the temple, most likely.

He gingerly lifted an intricately carved dagger from the wall. Its grip formed an image that was reminiscent of an ankh. On each side of the handle was a tiny stone, red on one side, blue on the other.

George tucked it gingerly into the waistband of his trousers.

"It is good. We must go."

"No, wait." George had spotted an alcove to the left. Coats hung from hooks on the walls. There were shelves with shirts and trousers. On the floor, beneath the coats, he found what he was looking for. After picking up and inspecting several pairs, George found a pair of brown boots that fit him reasonably well. He put them on. "Alright, I'm ready. No, wait." He pulled on the stranger's sleeve to stop him.

"Yes?"

"Who are you?"

"Ungris."

"Well, what are you doing in this place? And what place is this anyway?"

The man removed George's hand from his shirt. "There is no time for your questions now. Not while we play for our lives. We must go."

"Don't you even want to know who I am? What I'm doing here?" demanded George, as if he himself knew.

"Come, George," said Ungris. "There is no time." He crossed the armory, stepping over the dead giant on his way out.

George hesitated only a moment. How had Ungris known his name? Had his captors told him? If so, how had *they* known his name?

The two men left the way they'd come. Ungris ran to the end of the corridor which ended at yet another corridor that ran right to left. He stuck his head around the corner then beckoned George on.

George tried to remember the turns. Left, straight down a passage to the left, straight past a bisecting corridor, right, right.

"This way!" Ungris continued their fast-paced escape.

As the two men rounded yet another corner, there came a sharp cry of surprise. A man brandishing a long blade ordered them to stop. When they did not, he raised a slender silver whistle to his lips and blew a high-pitched signal; three sharp bleats.

Ungris pushed George back and yelled. "Our way is blocked. Run, George, run! Back the way we came!"

George bolted, desperately trying to remember the way they'd come but it was no use. Even in the best of times, he'd never have held all those twists and turns in his memory. The sounds of shouting grew louder. It seemed as if an entire army was chasing them.

Ungris stopped in the middle of the long corridor and faced down their lead attacker, a nasty looking thug with a black face and black eyes.

"What are you doing?" cried George.

"Go! Right, then another right Then follow the next corridor. There is another way that will lead you through the kitchen to the garden."

"But what about you?" The light in the distance was growing brighter. It sounded like another dozen footsteps or more heading their way.

The soldier was upon Ungris now, swinging his wide blade in a cutting arc towards his head. George watched helplessly.

Ungris bent his wrist and parried. "I will find you. Go, George! There," his blade bounced off the other's and thrust out, "is," his opponent countered," no," Ungris grunted as the blade cut a path that a few centimeters further would have relieved him of his arm, "time!"

George nodded and ran.

Left, right, right. No, right, right, left. Damn. He had no idea. Did that last corridor go right or both ways? Was he supposed to count that? Damn, Ungris, he should have been clearer.

A gray dressed giant appeared before him. His head was large and uneven as a boulder that had been bouncing aimlessly around the earth for a millennia or two. His smirk, ringed by thick purple lips, was like a hideous, open wound.

George ducked as the giant's long, thin fingers grabbed for him, tearing his shirt. He tumbled and launched himself backwards. He found a door and hurried inside, slamming it shut behind him. George grabbed a low table and shoved it in front of the door.

The giant banged on the door and howled, sending a cold shiver up George's spine. He quickly surveyed the room. There was a huge table in the center, surrounded by tall chairs. This had to be the dining hall.

Tapestries, more works of madness by the look of them, hung suspended from the walls. Dropping from the ceiling on a rough iron chain, with links as thick as his thumbs, loomed a macabre chandelier decorated with skulls, yellow and scarred, holding crooked candles that smelled of lye. Some of the skulls looked human, others appeared decidedly inhuman, almost monkeyish. George couldn't take his eyes off the thing as he wondered what sort of mind had created an object so deplorable.

The giant's fist rammed through the door. He stuck his eye through the hole he'd made. "I hunger for you," he cooed. The giant blinked and rattled the door.

George backed away. There was no place to hide. He looked feverishly for an avenue of escape. The giant banged another hole in the door. It was only a matter of moments before he would be through.

George frantically pushed aside the thick tapestries. Was it possible to hide behind one? Could there be a concealed exit? Had Ungris gotten it wrong?

Heart bursting, George thrashed about for a way out. There had to be some escape besides his imminent death. Behind the fourth tapestry, George found what he was searching for. A doorway. He glanced across the room in time to see the giant's efforts reduce the door to splinters that exploded into the air like confetti.

The giant grinned like a demon. "Peek-a-boo," he cooed.

George fled. It was a kitchen, with massive stoves along both walls and a long, steel preparation table between them. Pots, pans and cooking utensils hung from an apparatus over the table. There was no obvious exit from here other than the way he'd come. The kitchen was L-shaped and George rounded the corner, praying for a door that would lead him out of this madhouse and preferably back to his own bedroom.

A low metal door, about a meter square, flew open in the wall beside him. Rough hands grabbed hold and threatened to tear him apart. George pounded on his attacker's arms.

In that same moment, an inhuman howl of victory split the air. George looked over his shoulder. The giant was coming!

"Get inside!"

George squatted to see who was mauling him. "Ungris!"

George let himself be pulled inside. Ungris began tugging on a rope that hung between his hands. The box they were in lurched upwards as the giant thrust in his arm. Ungris bashed it aside and shouted. "Close the door!"

"I can't. He's blocking it!" George pulled his legs further under himself, fearful that the brute would drag him out feet first.

"Then help me pull!" grunted Ungris.

George nodded and laid his hands on the rope. They pulled quickly. The giant's fingers grabbed the edge of the metal box they were riding in. Together, George and Ungris pulled with all their might. But the giant was strong.

"Watch out," cried Ungris. "And mind the rope. Don't let go." He swung his leg past George and stomped on the giant's fingers with the heel of his boot.

The giant wailed and released his grip.

Relieved of the giant's weight, the box shot quickly higher and Ungris returned to the rope.

"What is this thing?" said George.

"A conveyance for food and supplies. Now, pull."

Together they tugged, hand over hand, until the box bumped against a ceiling of sorts. They sat in darkness.

"End of the line," grumbled George. "Now what?"

"Quiet," cautioned Ungris. His hands fumbled along the side of the wall. He pushed. Light spilled into the box. He nodded and lowered himself through the opening; motioned for George to follow.

−16−

George quickly climbed out and straightened up. Relieved to be out of the dark confines of the miserable and cramped primitive conveyance Happy to discover they were in a glen of sorts, lightly wooded and surrounded by tall bushes bearing red and purple berries. There was a tang in the air, like cranberries, only darker somehow.

"What-what is this place?" demanded George.

"I do not know." Ungris' eyes glowed with anticipation. "Which way, George?"

George would have socked Ungris if he'd thought he could have gotten away with it. Fortunately there was another course of action that would probably have far more favorable benefits beyond venting his mounting frustration.

Like a bird reacting to bright colors, George succumbed to his appetite, ignoring Ungris and heading straight for the red and purple fruits. The leaves of the bushes were triangular and sticky to the touch.

George pulled a handful of red berries from the first bush he'd come to, rolled them around with his fingers, then popped them into his mouth. They were cool.

He bit down and liquid squished out into his mouth. The berries were tangy and sweet. George's empty stomach grumbled its satisfaction.

George sensed Ungris at his side. "Aren't you going to eat any?"

Ungris nodded. He snatched a handful of red berries from one bush and a near equal handful of the purple berries from another. He shook them up all together in his cupped hands then poured them into his mouth. He grinned, his cheeks swollen like an acorn-munching squirrel's.

Ungris chewed slowly, swallowed and wiped his juice stained lips on the sleeve of his shirt. "Why do you wait?"

"Wait?" said George as he idly picked a second handful of the red berries.

"Yes. If you do not eat the red nasters with the purple, the poison in the red can kill within minutes."

"What!" George's eyes filled with terror. "Why on earth didn't you tell me?"

George reached out for a cluster of so-called purple nasters that hung from a nearby branch. He broke it off at the stem and shoved the whole thing in his mouth, leaves and all. George masticated the berries quickly and swallowed even more quickly.

Ungris watched him and shrugged. "I thought you knew."

George spat out tiny bits of indigestible bush. "I hope I ate fast enough."

Ungris stroked his chin. "Hope never sleeps."

"And what the bloody hell is that supposed to mean? I could be dying any moment and you're reading me fortune cookie aphorisms."

"I apologize." Ungris bowed his head. "I am doing my best."

"Yes, well—" George didn't know what to say. This Ungris fellow sounded genuinely sorry. And Ungris had very probably saved his life back in that awful labyrinth. "Look, forget about it. But next time, warn me if you see me doing something stupid." He glanced at the red and purple berries with newfound respect. "Or deadly."

"Yes, George. With this in mind, I believe we should be going. After all, they know where we are."

George looked across the clearing to the little dumbwaiter of sorts that they'd ridden up in. "All right. Let's go."

"Oh, George?"

"Yes?"

"What is a fortune cookie?"

"A fortune cookie? You don't know what a fortune cookie is?"

Ungris shook his head.

"Well, how can I describe it?" George used his fingers. "They're these little cookies—kind of hard and sweet—with a bit of paper rolled up inside."

"Paper?" Ungris looked quite surprised. "You eat this?"

"No, no. You read it. It's your fortune."

"I see," replied Ungris, though he appeared not to; his brows squeezed together in thought.

George stalked off between a break in the tall bushes. Ungris walked behind him. "Are these good fortunes or bad?"

"Good, of course," said George. "Sometimes they're just silly. I mean, they make them up in a factory somewhere."

Ungris matched George's step and caught his eye. "You have a factory that manufactures good fortunes?" His dark green eyes swelled with wonder.

George nodded.

"You live in a wondrous place, George."

They spent the night at the edge of a clearing in the woods. Neither wanted to camp out in the middle, feeling they'd be too exposed there. Ungris produced a small fire and filled a sack with water from a nearby stream.

Lowering himself to a flat rock beside George, Ungris announced, "I saw the lights of Ryaii below the stream. We should arrive by morning. You have led us well."

George rolled his eyes. For all he knew, they had been wandering around Yellowstone Park somewhere. Maybe even Jellystone Park for that matter. He kept these admissions to himself. He shoved at the fire with a long stick, making the flames dance and sparks fly. "Tell me about those giants back there."

"Giants?"

"Yes, like that big fellow you killed in the armory. And

the other one who was chasing us."

Ungris' laugh broke the darkness. "Ah, you mean the Llorri."

"If that's what you call them."

"I did not kill the Llorri," said Ungris.

"But I saw you. Without a weapon, only your own two hands."

Ungris kept smiling. "One cannot kill a-a giant as you say, George. At least not a one such as I. No," said the squat man, shaking his head, "one can only slow them down."

"S-slow them down?"

Ungris nodded.

"But he was lying there. Dead."

"No, only incapacitated." Ulric took a swig of water. "I am certain he is up and about now. With a sore neck and in a foul mood." Ungris gazed out across the clearing. "In a mood to kill me should he get the chance, I'd reckon."

He jabbed a crooked finger at George. "You, too, I would reckon."

George trembled.

Smothering a yawn, Ungris said, "The Llorri do not like to be bested. It only makes them all the more determined. That one in Thudor's labyrinth has my scent now. He will not rest until he has destroyed me or been destroyed himself."

"Yet you said these Llorri cannot be killed—"

"Yes, that is so." Ungris' face broke into a flame lit grin. "Perhaps I shall need a fortune cookie, yes, George?"

George nodded. He could use a big one himself.

Somebody call the factory.

He wanted to ask Ungris many more questions, but his enigmatic travel companion had rolled over onto his side and closed his eyes.

George turned to the dying flames. He'd heard of seers who could see the future in fire. George wished he could and gave it a try. He saw only light, felt only heat. Watched embers glow red, turn to gray and disappear.

—17—

"I want the truth, Mother."

"What? What truth?" Mrs. Richards looked up, nervous. Everything was getting harder. Fixing meals, raising the kids, taking care of the office work.

"The truth about Dad," Tim said.

Mrs. Richards set down the potato peeler. What's the use, she thought, I've already cut my fingers twice. She opened the refrigerator and pulled out a carton of orange juice; poured herself a short glassful. "I don't know what you mean." Her voice quaked, weak and nervous.

"You know exactly what I mean!" Tim said loudly. "I want to know what you've done with Dad!"

"Shush. Timmy, keep your voice down." Mrs. Richards shot a quick look down the hall. "Claire might hear you."

Tim scowled and crossed his arms over his chest. "Claire is in her bedroom with the door shut playing on the computer. She's got the volume up so loud she can barely hear herself, let alone us, Mother."

He grabbed his mother's wrist. Orange juice leapt from her glass, splashed onto the counter. "Careful, Timmy, look what you've made me do."

"Mom, I am not a kid. I'm Tim. Call me Tim. And please, tell me what you've done to Dad."

Tim's eyes locked onto hers, pleading.

How she wished she could appease them. What mother doesn't want to appease her son?

"He's missing. Your father is missing, Tim." She turned away, to hide her fright driven tears.

"No, he's not. You're lying! Why are you always lying to me? Turn around, won't you? Face me. Are you afraid to face me and tell me the truth?"

Mrs. Richards said nothing. She covered her face with trembling hands.

"You've locked him up, haven't you? Locked Dad up just because he's different. Just because he isn't what you expect him to be—what you want him to be."

Tim's accusations stung to the bone. And he wasn't letting up.

"You had him committed. He's probably locked up in some stupid room in stupid Miami right now. You've got him so upset with everything that he's probably starting to believe he's crazy himself. You see what you've done?"

"Tim, I—"

Suddenly Claire was there, peering around the kitchen

island as if she was a whale just coming up for air. "Why is Tim yelling at you, Mommy?"

Tim saw his mother jump, clutch the counter. Her shoulders heaved uncontrollably, but she didn't turn around.

"I-I'm sorry, Mom. I didn't mean to yell." Suddenly, he felt like crying himself.

He took Claire's hand. "Come on," he said, forcing a smile, "I'll play Barbie with you."

Mrs. Richards waited until she heard the sound of their footsteps fade into nothingness. She pulled a paper towel from the rack and used it to wipe her eyes. Standing on a footstool, she pulled the vodka down from the high shelf over the microwave and poured it into her glass. Somehow, orange juice was just not enough anymore.

George tried to recall what he'd read about schizophrenia once and wondered how it applied to himself. The psychiatrists said it had something to do with splitting off of portions of the psyche. Sounded like a lot of Ph.D mumbo-jumbo to him but, according to them, people afflicted with schizophrenia often retreated into themselves, into a world of hallucinations and delusions.

Was that what was happening to him? Was this about more than just him locking himself up in a corner of his office where no one could see him? Had he taken it too far? Had he pushed himself over the limits of sanity and into a world of craziness?

If so, how would he return? As his mind worked, his

footsteps fought to maintain their grip on the tumbling rocks along the stream's edge as he and Ungris followed the track of the gorge towards Ryaii.

If he was truly mad, what hope did he have for recovery? Were the doctors working on him even now? George rubbed his arms up and down. Was Doc Grossman sticking i.v. needles and tubes filled with mind altering chemicals into his forearms in an effort to redirect him back toward the reality that most people shared?

George had to admit, he did have a decreasing attachment to the outside world; the world beyond his immediate family at least. He had few friends. None, actually. Hadn't since high school, truth be told. And very few acquaintances. He barely even shared more than a nod with any of his neighbors.

The gorge disintegrated into a thick wood which Ungris led them into without pause. It turned out to be deceptively shallow, like some facade created by theme park landscape designers.

In a matter of minutes, they were through. Though the street was not familiar to him, George recognized the roofs of Ryaii.

Oddly, it gave him a sense of homecoming to see those homes and buildings once again. Perhaps there was a way back to things lost. As Ungris had said, hope never sleeps.

Ungris marched into a tavern and George followed, compelled more by the scent of food than companionship. How odd that he'd suddenly found his appetite in this world. The tavern was wider than it was deep, with tables and chairs scattered about in clusters. There was a bar along the back. George smelled fried eggs.

Several heads turned to look. Their eyes were curious yet not unfriendly. On the left, a wall of what might have been slate contained a fireplace three times bigger than any George had every seen. Ungris and George took a table near the smouldering fire. A small woman brought them hot tea.

Ungris dipped two of his fingers into a pot of honey then used them to stir his tea. George, wondering how many unwashed fingers might have done the same, decided to drink his unsweetened. He took a sip, let the steam rise up to his nostrils. It tasted like green tea with a touch of cinnamon, maybe cherries.

The woman, with a widow's peak highlighting her black hair, brought out a basket of rolls. "Would you gentlemen need anything more?"

"No. Thank you," said Ungris, picking through the basket and plucking out a dark roll for himself. "Aren't you eating?"

George experienced a sharp pang of hunger, sharp as a knife. "I-I have no money with me."

Ungris laid some silver coins on the table. "Eat."

"But I can't pay you back."

"You are my guest and you would honor me."

George mumbled his thanks. Once more he was indebted to this stranger, just as he had been equally indebted to Cleea and Sharan. It made him feel awkward, vulnerable. Nonetheless, hunger called. He grabbed a sweet roll filled with raisins and chewed it ravenously.

Ungris was grinning at him. "You're an odd bird, George." Then quickly he added, "No offense."

George shrugged, his mouth stuffed with bread. It was the best he'd ever eaten; sweet and chewy. "None taken."

Ungris quickly gobbled up a second roll, something covered with sesame seeds. He refilled his own teacup after topping off George's. Ungris slowly surveyed their fellow diners before speaking. Softly, he said, "So, if you don't mind my asking, what were you doing in Thudor's place?"

George explained about the man he had been following and how he'd been taken by surprise, led to the storeroom and left there.

Ungris was shaking his head. "These are remarkable times, George. Thudor could never have gotten away with such a thing in Ryaii in the past." Ungris slammed his hand down on the tabletop. The table's spindly legs shook like it was having a heart attack. "He'd never have dared try!"

"Who is this Thudor, anyway?"

"You test me," accused Ungris. He didn't look too happy about it.

"Test you? How do you mean?"

Ungris wiped his mouth with the back of his sleeve. "You know quite well what sort of devil Thudor is. He is a minion of—"

"Of what?" George leaned forward. "Of who?" Ungris looked frightened. George was taken aback. The fellow had shown no fear back there at this lair of Thudor's, strangling giants and fighting off attackers with obviously murderous intentions. "What are you afraid of, Ungris?" He drove forward. "Who controls Thudor?"

Ungris' brow broke out in sweat. "I-I cannot say. If you test me, so be it. But I will not say."

George couldn't understand what was going on. Ungris actually sounded angry with him. But why? And what was he so afraid of?

"It is too much to even think his name. To say it," Ungris shook his head, "to say his name is to invite his presence." Ungris stiffened his back. "I will not do this. It is too dangerous."

Ungris shot to his feet. "We should go, George. We have nourished ourselves and there is no time."

George stood, swilled the last of his dregs, stuck an extra roll in his pocket and headed for the door.

After several turns, they came to a narrow rising street that George recognized at once. Though he'd initially been brought to this place unconscious, it was from here that he'd then followed the strange man, without knowing he was being led, all the way to Thudor's trap.

George stopped outside the door. He rubbed the cottage wall. Its surface was chalky. "How did you know to lead me here?"

"I did not. I could not lead you, George. I only accompany you back. How could I lead when I do not know where you go?"

These people are all nuts, thought George, opening the

door without a thought to knocking.

Sharan rose to greet him. "George. I am glad you have returned. You should have waited for me. You gamble much."

"Sorry," George said. It seemed as good a thing to say as anything.

"Thank you for your assistance, Ungris."

Ungris bowed. "It was my honor."

"You two know each other?"

"Yes," said Sharan gathering up her pack and two others. She handed one to George and the other to Ungris. "Come, there is no time. The others are waiting."

Waiting for what, George wanted to know, longed to ask—but Ungris and Sharan were already moving out the door.

What was that saying? There is no rest for the weary. George decided to add an amendment. There is no rest for the certifiably mad.

Sharan headed uphill. After a hundred meters or so, the road emptied into a square into which three other roads likewise converged. In the center of the square rose a fountain of blue stone from which a single plume of clear water rose; its gurgle barely audible.

Opposite them rose an immense—at least on the local scale—gray, granite edifice with a gabled roof. The roof shimmered and flowed like liquid glass. A single spire disrupted the otherwise austere roof line. A pair of massive black doors fixed into stilted arches stood at the end of a wide row of granite steps leading upward. There were no windows visible.

George felt a sense of power emanating from the impressive structure and he was awed by it.

Sharan's path led them directly past the blue fountain and George could have sworn he heard voices, small whispers, coming from the water—calling to him in words that lit on his brain like hummingbirds' feathers. What were they trying to tell him?

Ungris and Sharan were at the steps of the big building. George hastened to catch up, leaving the whispers behind. "What is this place?" he said softly to Ungris as he huffed up the shallow, flat steps.

"This is the Seat."

The young woman, Sharan, stood before the black doors. They towered over her like twin black holes. And like black holes, the doors offered back no light, no reflection, no blemish.

Sharan extended her arms out and down, palms facing the doors.

"What is she—"

What George saw next seemed unbelievable. The doors did not open, they simply disintegrated. First there had been a quick shimmering, like a wave of energy pulsing through them. Then a blur of smoky gray appeared in the center of each door, congealing and growing until only emptiness remained.

George stepped forward. What he now saw equally made

no sense. For he saw himself! It was like looking into a blue-bottomed swimming pool and seeing a reflection of one's self. He saw himself, but not Ungris and not the girl.

Had everything but himself disappeared? No, a glance to his side told him that Ungris and Sharan still stood before him. But they were not visible in the doors.

He swivelled.

The square still existed. The blue fountain still flowed. Others were moving about. But none were reflected in the black doors which had become mirrors.

Ungris stepped forward. He passed through the liquid mirror like a drop of color being absorbed into a glass of water.

"Come, George," said Sharan. She held out her hand.

"Where did he go?"

"He waits for us in the Seat. Come. We will join him."

George hesitated. He didn't relish dissolving into a-a who knew what. "How come I can't see you?"

"What?"

George pointed. "How come I can't see you? In there."

"Ah. The eyes of the Seat see us each in our entirety. We are seen only to ourselves, separately, for who we are. Never more, never less. We may only see ourselves through the eyes of the Seat, never another. This would not be just.

"The eyes of the Seat see through us and, if what they see is good, in return allow us to see through them. Only the eyes of the Seat can do this. Though perhaps it is different for you?"

George shook his head no. How could he explain that where he came from the doors were far more pedestrian; they kept out the cold and strangers at best.

He took Sharan's offered hand and allowed himself to be led forward, wincing as they passed into the eyes of the Seat. He felt a chill tingling as they swept through.

The fierce light on the other side burned his eyes and George threw his hands up in the air to block the unexpected glare. Despite the intensity of the light, it was as gelid as the space between the stars.

Sharan was grinning. "It is beautiful, is it not, George?"

"I wouldn't know," complained George. He was squinting fiercely and still couldn't bear to look higher than Sharan's knees. "Can't somebody turn down the lights?"

Sharan laughed. "Who but you could say such a thing? The eyes of the Seat see well."

"Tell me," said George, wiping tears of pain brought on by shafts of brilliant light that jabbed his eyes like a thousand hot needles, "what happens if the eyes of the Seat don't like what they see?"

"They do not let such a one pass," Sharan replied, her expression turning sober.

"Meaning?"

"Meaning," answered Sharan, "that such a one would not be permitted to continue in their existence."

George's forehead scrunched up like a wizened concertina. Then he understood. "You mean dead, don't you?"

He gazed at the massive doors. The square outside was clearly visible though no sound penetrated his ears. He was pointing. "Those things would kill him, wouldn't they?" His voice rose. "They might have killed me! I mean, for all you know, I could be dead now."

Ungris had said you couldn't kill a giant, but what would happen to one of those giant Llorri if he should dare to attempt to pass?

Sharan looked unfazed. "Do you believe in death, George?"

"I—" George stopped himself. At that point, he didn't particularly believe in life or death, so why bother arguing about it with her?

In a gesture of defiance, he turned away to avoid further discussion. "My God—"

The ceiling above them looked as far away as all eternity and still close enough to touch. Like a giant lens, translucent and white, stretching out above and beyond. It was impossibly large. Too large to exist within the building they had entered.

Embedded in the center of the floor was a vibrant circle of lustrous stones—an irregular deep blue one, the size of George's fist, surrounded by five smaller, yet equally irregular, brilliant red ones. George noted that the blue stone was the same color as the fountain outside. Were they made of the same material? What did it all mean?

"Beautiful, is it not?"

"It's an illusion," snapped George.

Sharan had taken his side. Her neck craned upward as if her face were a flower seeking to soak up the life giving energy of the sun. "It is the Eye of the World," she said solemnly.

George nodded as if that meant something to him.

Sharan started down a sharp black slope that ended in a depression several meters below. Ungris was there.

So was Cleea.

George nearly shouted out in response to the unexpected joy that swelled up within but, with effort, resisted the temptation. How could he express any joy here in this place? In this world? How could he feel any joy when he'd been driven from his own world and into this incomprehensible one?

Cleea approached. Unlike the blue fountain, the Eye of the World gave off a virtual roar like a billion billion whispers joining together in some thunderous voice that jostled George's ears so vibrantly he felt the tender little bones would shake loose.

Yet when she spoke, she spoke softly, and he heard her clearly. "Hello, George."

Her clothing was fresh, clean, but still the same style of dress she'd first worn when he'd initially encountered her. When? Was it a lifetime ago?

It was as if George was standing beneath Niagara Falls and a colossal hand had suddenly, momentarily shut off the water. "Hello, Cleea."

For a brief second, Cleea's eyes betrayed a layer of

weariness and, perhaps, fear? And then she smiled. "It is wonderful, isn't it, George?"

"If you say so." George felt vertiginous, as if standing ungrounded over a deep, yawning inky void. At any instant, he expected to plummet through an endless, dizzying wormhole. "What's it supposed to be? What's it supposed to mean?"

"Mean, George?" repeated Cleea.

"Yes, what does it do?"

Cleea came closer. "We keep watch and ward on the World Soul." She extended her right hand high. "Can't you see?"

George's eyes fought against the light. The weight of the sight seemed to push him down. "I don't see anything," he oathed. "I don't even know what I'm supposed to see."

"Everything."

"Everything?" George looked at Cleea skeptically.

Sharan interjected. "The Eye of the World sees all. It is up to the viewer to see what he or she wishes to see—must see."

"That's ridiculous," replied George.

Ungris gasped as if George had shouted sacrilege.

Encouraged by Ungris' reaction, George marched on. "Look, I don't know why you brought me here. I admit it's a pretty enough sight. But I've seen better special effects at Disneyworld."

Cleea spoke softly. "Give me your hand, George."

George hesitated, then stuck out his left hand.

"Now," said Cleea, "close your eyes and think about what

you wish to see. Are you doing this?"

George grunted.

"Good." Cleea squeezed his hand. "Now, slowly, slowly open your eyes and look up through the Eye of the World. Slowly. Remain focused on what your mind sees."

George held on to the image of his wife and children that he'd conjured up inside his battered brain. Doing as Cleea said, he opened his eyes a mere crack at first and craned his neck upward to the Eye.

Finally, his eyes opened fully and he forced himself to look at the blinding light. "I don't see—" George's breath caught in his throat.

It was Claire! Sitting in her room. But how? And there was Tim, sitting in a chair in the family room. God, his son looked awfully forlorn.

Then he saw Elaine. She was in the bedroom. Standing in front of the bathroom mirror. Crying her eyes out. Her skin was puffy. Her shoulders sagged. She looked like she'd been bearing the weight of the world.

The images of his family grew clearer, drew nearer to one another as if compelled by a subatomic bond.

George felt a searing stab of pain in his gut. The images of Elaine, Tim and Claire shattered like cheap glass in a hurricane.

Ungris cried out. Cleea and Sharan were shouting.

A black dot appeared near the center of the Eye, pulsating and growing.

Hi-el, George. Hi-el. Remember, George. Fear, George.

The black spot winked out.

George slumped to the ground, bathed in a cold, penetrating sweat. "Get me out of here." He crawled on his hands and knees towards the edge of the black bowl, seeking its lip.

And escape.

Hands reached under his armpits and lifted him. It was Sharan and Cleea. They climbed, against the darkness below them and the brightness above, they climbed. George was half-carried, half-dragged along a black tunnel that emptied into a large, domed rotunda.

They set him gently in a cushioned blue velvet chair. George gripped the arms tightly.

"Are you all right, George?" Cleea laid her hand on George's damp forehead.

He nodded.

Cleea said, "Perhaps you thirst?"

George fought back a snide remark. The only thing he thirsted for was going home. Still, he didn't fight it when Sharan left the room and returned with a pitcher of water and a glass.

He drank—the water was icy as a mountain stream—and then asked, "What is going on? Are you trying to kill me?"

Cleea knelt beside him. "No, George. Of course not. You are our friend. Our hope." She rose, her face wrought with agitation and paced the chamber. "I do not understand. He has never come this far. His power grows beyond our expectations and predictions." She slammed her fist into her opposite palm. "There is no time."

Gee, where have I heard that before? thought George. Funny, all his life there had been nothing but time. Too much time. And these people or angels or lunatics or figments of his insane imagination kept saying how there was no time!

"He who?" demanded George, rising unsteadily on his feet. "You mean Hiel, whoever he is?"

Sharan gasped.

Cleea calmed her. "It is best not to—"

"How did he know my name?" He looked from one angel to the other. "What does he want with me?"

"He spoke to you, George?" said Cleea.

"Yes, you heard him."

The angels shook their heads.

"What? You're joking? It was so loud, nearly deafening." They looked puzzled.

George looked about madly. "Where's Ungris? He was there. He heard him, too. We all heard him."

"Ungris is not with us now," answered Sharan.

"He has other paths," added Cleea, mysteriously.

"But Hiel said his name and he told me to remember." George massaged his stomach, remembering the exquisite, inhuman pain. "He told me to fear."

Cleea replied. "We heard nothing. We only saw the darkness."

"Hiel grows stronger," said Sharan. "Bolder."

Cleea nodded solemnly. "Cloudja is in greater danger than we knew."

"Who is this Hiel?" repeated George. "And, for that matter, who or what is Cloudja?"

Cleea came to his side. "Why do you ask questions when in your heart you know the answers, George?"

He waited in a posture of defiance.

"Cloudja is Queen of Ryaii and Guardian of the Eye of the World," began Sharan, with a voice that could not mask its reverence.

"Hiel," said Cleea, taking up the explanations, "is the Lord of the Deep Refuge. He wishes to subvert the Eye."

"If he succeeds, it will be the end," whispered Sharan, her voice painted with fear. "The end of it all."

—18—

"Merry Christmas!" Mrs. Richards forced a smile.

She felt as if she was stuck in a border town along the tormenting edge of Hell, but she was determined to keep up a good face on things—for her children's sake.

"Merry Christmas, Mommy," said Claire, resting on the edge of the couch. Her toes squiggled. She clutched her bulging Christmas stocking.

"Yeah, Merry Christmas, Mom," echoed Tim.

Like always, the tree stood tall as a mountain and the gifts, like always, rose seemingly to its peak.

But unlike always, there was an air of emptiness to the room. To the house. To the planet.

"Well," Mrs. Richards clapped her hands, "who wants to open the first present?"

"I will." Claire hurried to the tree and grabbed a red and blue package with her name on it. She'd been eyeing it for nearly two weeks.

"I wonder what it is," said her mother.

Claire tore off the paper. "It's the antique doll I wanted. The one Daddy told me was too expensive!"

"Cool," said Tim.

Mrs. Richards gasped. It was the antique Kewpie doll that Claire had been dying for. She didn't know how or when he had found it. He had kept it a secret from her. That was just like him. He liked surprises that put smiles on the faces of others.

A lot of these presents were collected by George before he'd. . .disappeared. She didn't even know what lay beneath many of the wrappings. Oh, George, why don't you come back? Why haven't the police found you?

The phone rang. Mrs. Richards jumped, turned and stared at the telephone on the kitchen counter.

It rang and rang.

"Aren't you going to get that, Mom?"

"What?"

"Mom, aren't you going to answer the telephone?"

"I'll get it," said Claire, racing to the kitchen. "Maybe it's Daddy!"

"What?!" Mrs. Richards leapt to her feet. "Wait, I'll take it." What if it was George, calling to wish them all a Merry Christmas from wherever he was? She couldn't let Claire face that.

She lifted the receiver, slowly, to her ear; afraid of what or who she might hear. "Hello?" she asked softly.

There was a long silence and then the sound of a disconnect. The dial tone hummed in her ear like a nervous mosquito.

"Who is it, Mom?" Tim was hovering over the counter.

Mrs. Richards turned. Her face was pale. Her eyes were hollow and sunken. She had been looking like this for days. "Wrong number," she said hoarsely. "Only a wrong number."

Had that been George on the other end, whispering her name? Had she really heard a voice at all?

Mrs. Richards closed her eyes. She felt lightheaded and couldn't breathe. Was she going insane? She felt a tug on her arm and opened her eyes. It was her daughter.

Claire pulled her mother back to the Christmas tree. "Let's open more presents, Mommy. I want you to open up one of yours from me next."

Mrs. Richards manufactured a small smile and wore it bravely as her precious, young daughter handed her a gift.

"I made it myself," boasted Claire.

Mrs. Richards opened the slender package. It was a drawing of— "It's lovely, Claire." She turned the picture sideways for a second look. "What is it supposed to be exactly?"

Claire turned the picture around and held it out proudly. "It's an alien world."

"Alien world?" Tim said, giving the drawing a skeptical once over. It was done on black construction paper with an inch wide red construction paper frame. There was something like a big white sun at the top. Crazy looking creatures—a giant bird that looked like an archaeopteryx, big turtles, delicate angels and more were arranged below in mad fashion. Like she was some kind of junior Salvador Dali.

Coming out of the sun was some sort of black chariot commanded by a rider in what was probably supposed to be black armor, like a maleficent knight. Claire had really outdone herself. Why couldn't she just draw Santa Claus like a normal kid?

"Uh-huh. You get to it by going under the ocean."

"The ocean?" Mrs. Richards said.

"That's just weird," said Tim.

"No it's not. I dreamed about it. Daddy's there. With the angels."

She pointed to a spot on the paper and Tim's eye followed. Sure enough, that did sort of look like Dad standing next to some tall angel.

Mrs. Richards gave out a startled cry. Claire's drawing left her hands and fluttered to the floor.

Tim made a face "You're crazy."

"Tim!" shouted Mrs. Richards.

"Sorry," mumbled Tim. Crazy was not a word to be used under any circumstances. Mom was sensitive about that. He knew better. But still, what Claire was saying, that was nuts! Where did she come up with this stuff?

"That's okay. I don't mind what you say, Tim." Claire retrieved her drawing from the floor and handed it back to her mother. "You should keep it someplace safe." She looked at her mother with eyes that belied her age. In a serious whisper, she spoke, "I don't want the Devil to get it. I don't want him to find Daddy."

Mrs. Richards nodded, held her daughter's picture in her trembling fingers. She felt like she'd been entombed in ice.

"And just how do I fit into all this?" demanded George. He felt his strength, such as it was, returning. The cold water had seemed to put out the flames that had ruptured his belly. But the mere thought of that hot whip searing into him started him quivering.

"We appeal to you, George," answered Cleea.

"You must lead us," chimed in Sharan.

"Lead you?"

Sharan nodded.

"Lead you where exactly?"

"Into battle," Sharan said, matter-of-factly.

"Into—" George was half out of his chair.

Cleea spoke. "Even now the forces of Thudor are agminated at the Steppes of Orexis."

George's abrupt laughter startled the angels. He jumped up, waving his arms. "You two ladies are crazy!" He jabbed himself in the chest. "I'm crazy." He waved his arms in a big arc. "We are all crazy," he said in slow, even tones. "Don't you see?"

Sharan and Cleea looked confused.

"I'm-I'm lying in a bed. A nice white bed, with Velcro straps all around so I don't fall out or run away and hurt myself." George looked over his shoulder and back again. "Doctor Grossman is back there. Watching."

George waved to the blank wall. "Yes, he's watching. I'll bet Elaine is watching, too. Hello, Elaine! Hello, Doctor Grossman! Hello, hello. Helloooo!" He was waving like a madman.

He turned to Sharan and Cleea. "I'd like you to meet a couple of friends of mine, Cleea and Sharan. These lovely angels are figments of my imagination. It's no wonder they are as mad as I, is it?"

"George—" began Cleea. She stepped towards him.

He backed away from her.

"Are you well?"

George laughed again. "Well? Of course I'm not well. I'm crazy. You've picked a crazy man to lead you on a crazy quest!"

"No, George," said Cleea, her voice was soft as the beds of Heaven. "We called you and you came because we needed you."

George's face turned hard. He shook his head. "No. I heard voices and I jumped in the fucking ocean." He slapped his thighs. "Can you believe it? God, I really am crazy! I heard voices and jumped in the ocean and dove and dove and dove—"

He paused. Then shook himself. "And then. . .I don't know. I must have passed out or something. Someone found me and now—"

George spun in a circle. "Here I am. Looneyville."

Cleea spoke with a voice of calm. "I know it has been difficult for you, George. You come a long way to aid us. You sacrifice much."

"You don't know my life." He considered his previous existence, spending his days tucked away in his hidey-hole of a cubicle; a gray life in a gray world. "Or do you?" He studied Cleea and Sharan closely. "Are you two angels?"

"Angels, George?"

"I heard angels in my head. You say it was you who was calling me. You're the angels, aren't you? So why are angels calling me?"

"As I told you, George. We need your help."

"Angels need my help?" George sounded skeptical.

"What is an angel, George?" replied Cleea. "To us, you are the angel."

George was shaking his head. "I got out of bed because I heard the angels in my head. I drove to the ocean like the voices told me to—"

"Yes, that was our calling," said Cleea.

"And I took a boat and rowed out into the ocean and, somehow I-I knew when I had reached the right spot and I-I jumped in. And I couldn't breathe and I couldn't see. There was so much light, bright, bright light. . ."

A fresh line of sweat had broken out on his forehead. "Am I drowning? Now?"

"No, George. You came to us when we called you. We knew that you would. You said you would."

"It was the Eye, George," spoke Sharan. "You came

through the Eye of the World."

George thought about what she was saying. The bright light. Could that have been it? Could he have been swimming towards the light and come through it somehow? God, they were sucking him into their fantasy.

He asked, "Then why didn't I come through here, at the Seat as you call this place?"

"The Eye is greater than what we see, George," answered Cleea. "You were where you were meant to be."

"And you just happened to be there when I arrived?"

"I was sent to meet you."

"So," said George, "what happens now, huh? What am I meant to do next?"

"You are meant to defeat the Lord of the Deep Refuge," Sharan answered quickly.

"You mean. . ." George thought of the monstrous beast who'd been slaying him in his dreams, over and over, flaying him alive as if in an ancient Aztec blood ritual, inch by exquisitely painful inch.

"Hiel," said Cleea solemnly. "And there is no time. You saw how he usurped the Eye."

George wanted to laugh, but Sharan and Cleea looked so serious, he dared not. He wondered if there were any offices in this place, some room with a nice little corner cubicle would do nicely right about now. Something without a window, without a phone, without visitors and without color. Without voices. He could use a hidey-hole.

The deep sounds of a bell resonated throughout the

rotunda.

"It is time," Sharan said.

"Yes, the Assembly is gathered. Please, come, George," urged Cleea.

George stared at the two angels a moment. For a second he almost thought he saw an image of his family hung between them on a chimerical glass they might have held in their angelic hands.

Was the key to seeing Claire, Tim and Elaine hidden in that illusory glass? Was there anything to do but go forward?

George nodded curtly and followed.

Two angels George had never seen before stood outside a horseshoe arched stone entry. They were weaponless but appeared to George quite vigilant and somehow eminently capable of stopping any person or creature that they did not wish to pass between them.

George and his companions entered a deep room which was ringed with tiers of stone seats that rose four stories into the air. Like the rest of the place, it was as cold as a deep freeze. This didn't seem to bother the angels who wore, like Cleea, simple and minimal clothing. Through the dim glow of light orbs placed at regular intervals along the wall, about two and a half meters up, George could see that the seats were full. Hundreds of eyes stared down at him as he entered.

Cleea, Sharan and he stopped in the center of the room.

"What is this place?" whispered George.

"This is the Ear," Sharan whispered back. "We listen to

the world here."

Cleea raised a hand and Sharan fell silent.

George noticed Ungris sitting two rows up, leaning forward. It was good to see a somewhat friendly looking face in the crowd. The rest were strangers. Some were similar to Cleea and Sharan, others were like Ungris. Still others were of vague and unrecognizable shapes, made all the more so by the shadows that partially obscured them.

"My friends," began Cleea, she spoke in a normal tone, yet her voice carried throughout the room, amplified by the acoustics of the design and materials, "these are grave times. The world as we know it, as we cherish it, has come under attack. Hiel," a murmur spread through the assembly, "Lord of the Deep Refuge seeks to control the Eye of the World. He seeks to control the World itself."

Despite his own disbelief, George found himself caught up in Cleea's strong words.

"Even now, Thudor, minion of Hiel, gathers his army at the Steppes of Orexis. Lives are in peril." Her voice was strong, and carried the strength of her heart in her words. "We must act."

There was a murmur of agreement from the Assembly.

Cleea raised her arms. "We have called." She turned towards George. "He has come."

The Assembly rose. There was thunderous applause.

Everyone was looking at George.

–19–

Time seemed to stop.

A bead of sweat rose on George's forehead like an eruption. "Leave me alone!" he shouted. He swirled and balled up his fists. "Leave me alone!"

George turned and fled the rotunda.

Cleea hurried after him. She caught up to him as he pushed through the Eyes of the Seat and hastened out-of-doors. "George, what ails you?"

George hurried on, drawn to the oddly compelling blue fountain in the center of the square. An ageless looking couple sat on a silver bench near the edge of the encircling walkway.

"George?"

"I'm drowning." George watched the waters dance. They danced as if they existed only for that moment—for that moment and for him and him alone.

He spun about, holding Cleea's gaze. "I am drowning," he said slowly. "Don't you get it?"

Cleea's raised brow made it clear she did not.

"I fell, or jumped in the ocean and I am drowning." He shook his head as if it would shake loose some answers. "I am drowning or I am already dead. Either way. I suppose it doesn't make any difference."

He waved his hands through the air. "None of this is real. You aren't real. I'm not real. Hiel is not real." Though remembering the vivid touch of Hiel's burning whip, it had surely seemed real enough.

George clutched Cleea's arms. "I cannot help you. I cannot save you." He hung his head. "I can't even save myself."

"You will not help us?"

George let go of Cleea's arms. "I can't. I can't help you. Don't you understand? I have no power. No magic. No weapons. Nothing. See?" He held out his empty hands. "Do you know what I do all day?"

Cleea shook her head.

"I sit in a little gray cubicle in the corner of my office and work. Hell, mostly I just try to stay awake. I stick these fucking little pieces of foam in my ears and the goddamn doctors talk about how sick their fucking patients are and I'm supposed to type it all up on the computer and send it back to them. Oh, what fun. Oh, what joy.

"Now, don't you think that if I had any magic powers that I just might do something else with my time? With my life, for crying out loud?" George paced along the edge of the fountain, whose waters whispered in his ears. What were they saying?

"Hell, sometimes I wish I only had enough power to end my life." He kicked the ground. "But I don't even have the strength for that." He sat at the edge of the fountain. "So how can I help you?"

"Do you cry out loud, George?"

"What?"

"Do you cry out loud?"

"Huh? What do you mean?"

"You said 'for crying out loud.' Do you?"

"It's-it's an expression. No, no I don't. Cry out loud, that is." Even as he answered Cleea, he wondered if he was speaking the truth. Was he crying out loud? Is that what his life was? Had become?

George's shoulders sagged wearily. God, he wished he could go home.

"You can if you want to, George."

"What?"

"You can go home."

"How did you know what I was thinking—what I wanted?" He clutched his head.

Cleea stood tall. "It is clear, George. We called you and you came. If you wish to leave, to return, that is your choice."

"What will you do?" George stood. "I mean, what about Thudor and this Hiel creature?"

"We will fight them."

"Can you defeat them?"

"That is not our decision."

"In other words, you might all be killed. Can this queen of yours really be worth it?"

"It is more than that, George. Cloudja is but one. She is the Guardian of the Eye of the World. Yet, the entire world is at risk. You saw yourself how Lord Hiel befouled the Eye. He stirs from the Deep Refuge. Soon, if we do not succeed in stopping him, he will be upon us all. And the world will be his."

"And so you would let yourselves be killed to stop him?"

Cleea looked at him steadily. "This is who we are, George. This is what we are."

George turned and stared at the fountain a moment. Billions of voices seemed to be whispering to him, tickling his ears with their myriad tongues. What were they saying?

"Tell me something," George said, with his back to Cleea, looking up at the fountain's nadir and the sky beyond.

"Yes, George?"

"Where is the sun?"

"In the sky where it always swims."

George's eyebrows rose. "Why can't I see it, then? Why haven't I ever seen it since I got here, since I arrived in this land?"

"How can you see that which is not there, George?"

George chuckled. "Of course. I should have known." George turned heel and headed across the square.

"George," called Cleea, "where are you going?"

"Back inside," replied George, loudly. "Hurry up, would you?"

Cleea ran to catch up. "You mean you will aid us, George?"

He looked into Cleea's eyes as they marched up the steps to the Seat. "Are you kidding? I wouldn't miss this for all the world." George was grinning like a madman. *For all the world.* That was exactly what he'd lost—the world.

George walked through the pulsating Eyes of the Seat without even slowing. "Fry me or free me," he mumbled, stepping boldly over the threshold.

Ungris stood, feet planted firmly at shoulder width, just inside the entry. "So, you've come back."

George felt Cleea's presence behind him. "Yes."

"Hiel," Ungris paused and looked over his shoulder as if half-expecting a dark shadow, "will destroy you if he can."

George nodded somberly. "According to Cleea and Sharan, he'll destroy the world if unchallenged."

"And so you will help us defeat Thudor's armies at Orexis and thwart Hiel's intentions?"

George shook his head. "I'll go with you. But I can't help."

"What?" Ungris' voice turned hard. "You would let us die? Is that why you come? To watch our demise?"

"Ungris," admonished Cleea, "that is unfair."

Ungris bowed towards Cleea. "My apologies, Cleea."

"Besides, it isn't like that at all, Ungris," explained George. "I can't help you. I have no power. No ability. I sit behind a desk all day. The hardest thing I struggle to do all day long is stay awake. Fight the boredom."

Ungris' eyes drilled into George's. "I trust you shan't be bored on this journey then. We face the destruction of our world, of our souls. Entertainment enough, I imagine, even for the likes of you." Ungris turned heel and disappeared down one of the Seat's unlit corridors.

George watched the bitter man go. He longed to call out to Ungris, explain to him that this was all a mistake, that there was nothing he could do. Yet he knew that Ungris would not understand, would not believe. Ungris, Cleea and the others suffered in a world of their own delusions just as he suffered in his.

The best he could do was to keep moving. Keep moving and see where it all led. Would it lead him to salvation? To answers? To sanity? Or would everything fade away in the end, in the blankness of death?

He'd read somewhere a theory that as a person died, time slowed down, slower and slower, until each moment became seemingly as long as a millennium and one's consciousness never reached that point where death became known. Perhaps that would happen to him. Perhaps it was happening even now.

He could be swirling around beneath the ocean right this minute, mere moments from eternal death, yet his mind stubbornly remaining alive in a world of its own creation, refusing to die. Refusing to face death. And thus, never recognizing it when it finally comes.

And it would come.

Would death announce itself?

Would he recognize it?

George marched to the rotunda. It was empty. "Where is everyone?"

"They have gone, George."

"It's just as well. I've nothing to tell them that is going to make them feel any better."

"You're wrong, George. Their hearts are lifted by your presence. Their strength is increased. Sharan will take you back to your quarters. I will inform the others that you have decided to join our quest."

George nodded. Sharan appeared suddenly, from nowhere, as if created out of the force of his mind. Maybe she had. No matter. He followed her back to the room where he'd awakened his first day in Ryaii.

Along the way, he probed Sharan for answers. "Tell me, Sharan," he said, "why can't I see the sun?" He was looking for discrepancies, something which would suggest whether any of this world he was experiencing was real. He was searching for the inconsistencies of dreams.

Sharan halted in her steps. "You cannot see the sun, George?"

George looked up at the blue-gray fuzz of sky. "No."

"Ah," Sharan nodded. "I understand. You look for it above."

"Of course I look for it above. Why the hell shouldn't I?"

"You must look beyond, George. Not merely above." She

resumed her steps and said merrily, "I'm sure you see it quite well now."

George craned his neck, looked up at the sky. He scratched his head. There wasn't a goddamn thing up there. Not even a bird. No moon. No clouds nearby. Though he had seen some scattered about earlier. If there was a bloody, ball of hot hydrogen gas floating about up there in the Beyond, it was beyond him.

Sharan rounded a bend in the road and George hurried to catch up.

"I have spoken with the Council and they in turn will notify the Assembly," announced Cleea, coming in through the curtained doorway, catching George as he slowly ate a long-needed meal in the presence of Sharan.

"So what happens next?" George pushed back his plate and stood. His stomach groaned, fuller than it had been in what seemed to be ages and the strong drink that Sharan had offered him warmed his heart. He felt suddenly drowsy.

"We have three days to prepare our ships for the journey. Fortunately, we have already begun the work and need only complete our provisioning. The Keepers arrive daily."

"Aye," said Sharan, "half of Ryaii seems to hold them now."

"Keepers?" asked George.

"Those who join the Quest and do battle against Thudor."

"Oh, you mean soldiers, warriors."

"In a manner, yes. But they fight only to preserve, never to destroy."

"What about Thudor and Hiel? Do you expect them to play nicey-nice?" George couldn't help but mock the seeming craziness of their position.

"No. It is not their way."

"Lord Hiel seeks to inflict misery and despair and, finally, death," put in Sharan.

In the face of Sharan's words, George regretted his mocking tone. He paced the room, finding his second wind in his indignation of Thudor, who'd already tossed him into a dungeon of sorts and Hiel, who'd been torturing him in dreams since he'd arrived. "So, tell me, why haven't you dealt with Hiel before? And what about Thudor? I mean, he's got that shop right here in Ryaii. I can take you there."

Cleea was shaking her head. "We had not the strength to face the Lord of the Deep Refuge until you arrived, George. As for Thudor, it is not that simple."

"How do you mean? It sounds simple enough to me. We go to that shop I was led to, knock down the door and drag out the bad guys." George snapped his fingers. "Boom, you're done. Job complete."

Sharan and Cleea were both shaking their heads this time. Cleea did the talking. "The door to Thudor's Keep is always changing. If we were to return to that shop of which you speak, do you know what we would find, George?"

"What?"

Cleea shrugged. "Only a shop. Nothing more."

George wanted to say that that was impossible. But then, everything about his recent experiences and, indeed this place, was impossible. "You're telling me the entrance is gone?"

"Yes," said Sharan. "Thudor's Keep lies in a between-place."

"A between-place?"

"A place between worlds and even time itself," replied Cleea.

Sharan added, "It is impossible to find access. We have tried through countless times."

"And yet you know how to find this Thudor at the Steppes of Orexis, or whatever you called it?"

"Yes," said Cleea. "That is the chosen place."

"Chosen by whom?"

"By Lord Hiel."

"How nice," replied George. "What did you do, make an appointment for this mass destruction like it was a hair appointment?"

"Hair appointment?" asked Sharan.

"Never mind," said George. He picked up the half-full bottle of something called brosia fr'Ryaii and poured himself a glass which he then quickly lifted to his lips. He sipped. The stuff had a distinct pomegranate flavor and strong wine kick. "Tell me, what is so special about this Steppes of Orexis? And why did Hiel choose it for this battle?"

"That is a question I can easily answer for you, George," responded Cleea. "The Steppes of Orexis are where the Eye of the World sees our defeat at the hands of Lord Hiel."

George quickly finished off his drink in an awkward gulp. It was just like his dream—that big, snake-like whip was going to tear him apart. In another place, in another time, he feared it already was happening. . .

"So, we are going to die," George said somberly.

"Perhaps," answered Cleea, "but only if we believe in it." Cleea extinguished the torch nearest the door. "We should rest now. In the morning, we shall inspect the ships. Sharan will show you your quarters."

George bade goodnight to Cleea and followed Sharan into another chamber. The building they occupied consisted of five circular chambers, the first of which held the door opening out to the street. This was a meeting room of sorts. In the center was the main kitchen. The other chambers were sleeping quarters, each with a small bath.

George looked about the room he'd been given. The conditions were Spartan at best. An economy lodge would have seemed luxurious by comparison, even without a TV set. This was not the same room he'd awakened in after collapsing out on the beach. But it would do. For sleep it would do just fine. With a little luck, he'd wake up in his own bed.

Just like in the movies.

–20–

"It's not your turn! Get back!"

Rabo stepped back, awkward and disoriented. The last thing he remembered, remembered with any certainty, that is, was driving down Avenue Rodrigues. He was late for work—he was a baggage handler—and there had been a roadblock on his way to the airport. He had been forced to turn around, crossing the busy road, looking for an open route to Aeroporto Galeão out on Ilha do Governador.

Ilha Pombeba had been floating tranquilly to his right. A city bus had appeared out of nowhere. He twisted the wheel and his car veered towards the water. He was moving too fast, but he'd hit the gas instead of the brake.

Now he was here, in a moment that had passed like a high speed camera shot, in a place he did not recognize or understand.

A young boy shoved him in the back. "Move forward,

fool!"

Rabo took a step forward. Bodies were pressed tightly all around.

"I'm going to be a chief one day," said the boy behind him.

Rabo turned.

"You see?" The boy held out his hands. They held dried strips of meat and fruits. He dropped the loose food down the front of his shirt. "And look, only three holes so far on my docket." He pulled a metal box, the dimensions of a pack of cigarettes from his back pocket and, using his thumbnail, pointed proudly to three small holes, that looked like they'd each been made by a metal hole-puncher.

Rabo nodded. He didn't know what was expected of him.

"How many have you got?"

Rabo followed the boy's gaze and was surprised to discover that his left hand held a similar brown metal box. A docket? It was like a thin metal sleeve, open at the top, and hollow within.

Rabo held out his box for the boy's inspection.

The boy's eyes widened. "You've got none?" He shook his head. "Man, I wouldn't want to be you."

No, you wouldn't, thought Rabo.

The girl ahead of them, with long stringy blonde hair was watching. She was thin and nearly as tall as Rabo himself. She had nervous eyes. The skin that masked her face was pale and gaunt.

"You believe this guy?" said the kid.

"How are you planning to get out?" Her eyes looked friendly, concerned.

"Get out?"

The boy quipped, "You want a trip to the surface, don't you? If you can't pay, how are you gonna get a trip?"

A man in a green uniform barked at them to keep their voices down. He held a device that looked like a cattle prod in his right fist and waved it in their direction to good effect.

Rabo felt his confusion turn to fear.

"You get to the front of the line with nothing to barter, they are gonna kill you, man,"prophesied the boy.

"But I don't—"

The girl pushed her hand up under her shirt and pulled out a fistful of food, papaya and coconut. A plantain. Take this." She shoved the food into Rabo's gut.

"I can't—Leave me alone." Rabo took a step back and bumped into the boy once again.

"Hey, watch where you're going," said the boy.

"Sorry." Rabo turned to the girl. She looked horribly malnourished despite the copious amounts of food that she was carrying around. She needed the food more, much more, than he. "Don't worry, I'll explain to them—"

"No," She was shaking her head. "You must, please," she pulled up the edges of his shirt, "before we are all punished."

"Yeah, hurry up, already" said the boy. "The guards are looking like they're ready to blow. You wanna get prodded? End up with a burning hole in your leg?"

"No."

"Then take it," urged Quill.

Rabo nodded quickly. He grabbed hold of the food as the line pushed forward.

"Smooth move, newbie."

"Thanks."

"I'm João," whispered the boy.

"My name is Rabo."

"This is your first time, isn't it?"

"Yes. I-I just got here." And he didn't even know where here was.

"No problem," said the kid. "I've been here plenty long. You watch me. You won't get killed. Like I said, I'm gonna be a chief someday. You'll want to know me—be my friend—if you know what's good for you."

Rabo studied the boy. He couldn't have been more than ten years old, half Rabo's age, and yet the kid seemed twice as smart. He'd keep that in mind.

The girl reached the front of the line.

"Hello, Quill," said the uniformed man at the turnstile. Beyond him, an olive-colored metal stairway rose, turned to the right, and rose some more. "Whatcha got?"

Quill emptied her shirt.

The guard nodded as he examined each bit of food. He scooped it all into a wicker basket beside him. "Not bad." He motioned for Quill to pass him her docket.

Over her shoulder, Rabo noted that hers was riddled with holes. The guard turned it over a couple of times, found a spot that he liked, extracted an electronic puncher from his belt and an instant later a pea-sized hole appeared.

Quill placed the docket back in the pocket of her blue jeans and nodded to Rabo. He gulped, handed the guard the food that Quill had given him, and extended his docket.

The guard eyed him for several moments. He carefully inspected Rabo's docket. Did he think it was a fake? That Rabo himself was a fraud?

In the awkward silence, Rabo shifted from foot to foot, trying to remember who he was, where he really was, and not think about this crazy world he'd ended up in.

Finally, the guard scooped the food into the basket atop Quill's offering, punched Rabo's card and motioned for him to pass through the turnstile. Quill was waiting for him on the other side. They headed up the stairs together and soon João joined them. There were guards stationed along the way, halfway up each stairway and on each landing.

After seven steep turns which left him breathless, Rabo reached the top. Several guards were loitering here, beside a bank of doors that looked like they had come directly from a decommissioned submarine. After a moment, one of the guards twisted the handle of one such door and pulled inward.

Quill stepped out first, then João. Only when one of the guards barked did Rabo join them. He hadn't known what to expect and still this was like nothing he could have anticipated.

They stood on a small metal platform in the Baía de Guanabara, edged by a metal railing. The platform swayed beneath their feet.

The wind was blowing and it was strong, nearly hurricane-like in force, whipping their hair about in a frenzy.

In the distance, Pão de Açúcar, Sugar Loaf, rose in all her glory. But surrounding her was a city unlike the Rio de Janeiro that Rabo had spent his life in and knew like the back of his hand. This was a city that might have been dreamed up by an inspired fantasy artist, of a far-distant Rio future with sharp-edged, shimmering skyscrapers that rose like alien spaceships across the horizon.

Gone were the brown favelas that colored Rio's edges and housed her poor. Where had they gone? All that remained was barren earth where millions had once lived and bred. . .and slowly, quietly starved, victims of their own being.

"The Uppers," whispered João.

Rabo heard the awe in the boy's voice. "Uppers?"

"We call them the Uppers because they live up here," replied the girl called Quill. "And because we live down there. You really are new, aren't you?"

Rabo nodded.

The boy, his hands clutching the rail tightly, said, "They're the uppers 'cos they got everything." One hand lifted from the rail and swept the air like a paintbrush. "Including all this. While we're stuck underwater—" There was bitterness in João's voice. "Like we're nothing but goddamn fish."

"João—" Quill said softly.

He turned. "It's true! We're nothing but goddamn little fishies to them. Nothing but guppies. Poor, hungry little guppies. And instead of sweeping us under their rugs, they've swept us off of their planet and into their fucking sea! But they'll pay. One day they'll pay." João's face hardened into a mask of hatred.

Rabo edged closer to Quill, farther from the door. "What is he talking about?"

"There is animosity between the Uppers and ourselves, the Lowers."

"You mean, like the upper class and the lower class?"

"Yes."

"I understand. Like the favelas, the slums?"

Quill nodded.

"What happened to them, anyway? I mean, millions of people live in the favelas."

"Lived," replied Quill. "That was ages ago."

"Ages?"

An alarm suddenly sounded. Lines appeared in Quill's forehead.

"What's that?" asked Rabo. "What's wrong?"

"Damn." João was pounding his fists against the metal rail that surrounded them. "It's not fair."

"What's not fair?"

"The outing has been cancelled," replied Quill. "We must return."

"Why?"

"Who knows?"

Rabo looked up at the brilliant tropical sky. It was deep blue; the clouds as billowing and white as the whipped cream his grandmother used to put in his hot cocoa. "You mean we have to go back? Down there?"

Quill nodded.

Rabo only then realized how claustrophobic a place the world below was. He wanted to stay up here, to feel the wind, smell the salty ocean air. He wanted to stay up here forever. The alarm, shrill and demanding, sounded in three quick bleats that brought pain to his ears.

"Hey, it's jammed!" João was hollering and pulling on the door's recessed handle.

Quill tried it too. They banged on the door together, knowing the guards would open it from the inside.

Rabo looked at the sea. Between the shores of the bay, a huge ocean liner, a skyscraper turned on its side, was approaching. The ship seemed to be half sailing, half flying through the air. And she brought with her a wake that was a good twenty meters tall.

It was headed their way.

He wanted to shout. To call out a warning to his companions. But his mouth refused and remained strangely silent. João and Quill looked up as the immense shadow of the ship flew overhead, bringing with it a black as deep as night.

"Watch out!"

That sounds like Quill, thought Rabo, out of a corner of his mind that seemed as distant as Reality. He felt himself being knocked bodily overboard. Swallowed by the great Water Monster. The sea was warm. He held his breath for as long as he could stand it. He was tossed, up, down, around and around until he could no longer discern which way was up and which way down.

When he could hold his breath no longer and the futility of staying alive became irrefutable, Rabo decided to let go. To go with the flow of the water, go with the flow of life and go even with the flow of death if he must.

Rabo opened his mouth and felt water rushing in, filling his throat. But to his surprise, he didn't die. In fact, he felt that he was breathing.

Rabo opened his eyes. Yes, he was still beneath the sea. Yet he breathed. He felt an odd tickling at the back of his neck. Groping behind his ears, he discovered something moving, fluttering. It frightened him at first. It felt as if some sort of creatures had attached themselves to him and were devouring him like a couple of giant slimy leeches.

Rabo was frightened for a moment, then the knowledge came to him—this was in reality his own body he was sensing. He had gills of some sort. And he was breathing!

He relaxed then, stuck out his arms and legs and let himself drift. Where were Quill and João? Were they breathing, too?"

Rabo floated along, as if he was the only life in the sea. It was an amazing world and Rabo wondered if it was real. Finally, he headed for the surface, attracted by a small boat that was drifting above him, no more than a dozen meters away. Her V-shaped hull cut a path parallel to his own. He turned and swam after her.

There was a short, teak platform at one end and Rabo angled towards it. As he lifted himself up, an older man wearing a white suit of clothing grabbed hold of his arms above the elbows. He was barefooted.

"Let go of me," said Rabo. "I can do it." Oddly, and with relief, Rabo discovered he could breathe just as facilely in the air.

"Nonsense, let me help." The man refused to let go and easily lifted Rabo onto the boat. His white suit seemed impervious to the water. His voice was as firm as ironwood timber.

"You shouldn't have done that," Rabo said, shaking himself. The boat was only ten meters long and no more than four at the beam and pitched vigorously in the rough seas.

"It is my duty to give succor," said the white-suited man. "I am Gason. I have the honor of meeting you."

"Well, Gason," said Rabo. "I am Rabo Ribeiro and I have the honor of having AIDS. So, you really might want to keep your hands to yourself."

Gason only smiled. He turned and Rabo noticed the boat's other passengers. Two women. One he didn't recognize, the other was Quill. They leaned against the side of the boat. One was wet. The other was dry. The dry one was smiling as if she knew something he didn't.

Rabo frowned. Nothing new there.

He studied Quill. The girl looked like she was in shock. Join the club, thought Rabo, who figured he'd be in a state of stuporous shock if he'd had half a brain and any good reason at all to worry about being alive, staying alive.

"What do you think, Cloudja?"

The woman rose gracefully. She was young and beautiful. Still, something about the way she bore herself signaled to Rabo that she was not a girl to be messed with or taken likely. He'd seen women like that before. They could be trouble.

This Cloudja woman had pale blonde hair which seemed to have strands of blue diamond woven in. Her long hair settled softly on her shoulders and the ends seemed to dance, as if by magic. She wore a white gown, apparently cut from the same bolt of cloth as this Gason fellow's.

"I believe we have found a link." She gazed at Rabo for a moment then wrapped her slender fingers over a cleat as she studied the sea. "Have we lost the boy?"

"I think not." Gason took the wheel and guided the small sailboat expertly.

Quill sat motionless in a puddle of seawater.

Two dozen ships, tall-masted, with hulls as sleek and black as seal skin, sat in the water. Cleea and Sharan had brought him to the harbor. The docks were bustling with workers loading the ships with supplies in long, sealed boxes.

George stepped to the edge of the nearest pier, avoiding a pair of women balancing a canoe atop their shoulders and making for one of the ships. "Canoes?"

"We'll need them later," said Sharan.

"When we leave the sea and cross the Forest of Nightfall upon the Rive Osfall," added Cleea.

"Terrific," grumbled George. His gaze followed the rhythmic rising and lowering of the waves that breached the shore. Somehow it made him feel homesick and created a pit of inquietude to his stomach.

"If we make it that far."

George turned. It was Ungris. He wore a gray uniform now with a blue belt. His blade was in a scabbard at his side. His boots were highly polished. "What do you mean, if we make it that far?"

Ungris grinned. "Death tempts us with every step. Draws closer with every breath."

"Ungris, please—" Sharan's voice was hard, scolding.

"Let him be, Sharan," said Cleea. "Ungris is only—" She paused, searching her vocabulary, "—cautious."

"You mean scared," taunted George.

Ungris puffed out his chest. "Of course I'm scared. Thudor taunts us freely, here in Ryaii. Even the Lord of the Deep Refuge dares to extend his touch. Scared? Yes, verily. But do not mistake me for a coward, none of you. I will do my share in this battle."

"We are certain of this," replied Cleea.

Sharan nodded.

"Aren't you scared, George? You should be." Ungris watched George's eyes as if the answer would reveal itself there long before his words did.

George took a slow breath and thought about Ungris' question. Was he scared? Probably. Scared of a lot of things. Scared of being stranded in this dream or other world, whatever it was. Scared of not going home. Scared he wouldn't see his kids again. Scared of ending up in that miserable little gray world of his, back in his little cage in his little office.

But was he scared of what lie ahead?

Memories of monstrous Hiel's whip mincing him came to surface. If he'd come to this place to die, then die he would. He looked deliberately into Ungris' eyes. "Yes, I'm scared."

George's words and smile caught Ungris off guard. "And since you all seem to think that I can help you or even save you, the very fact that I'm scared ought to scare the hell out of you."

He turned and marched away from the dock, leaving Ungris and the two women to their own devices. George followed the wide streets of Ryaii down familiar passages, until he arrived at the square of the blue fountain.

There was something oddly comforting about that fountain. He dipped his hands in the cool water in its basin and sat at the edge. Moments went by and then the whispers came, filling his ears with their songs and words; their poems and desires.

George closed his eyes and listened. He couldn't be sure, but he could swear that out of those millions and millions of whispers brushing past his ears, that he occasionally, just now and again, heard a word, a snatch of conversation, from Claire, Tim and even Elaine.

It wasn't much. But it was something.

He said nothing, yet his thoughts were filled with words,

and he wondered if his family heard them.

—21—

Tim was in his room.

The sky was dark, the world was growing quiet.

Christmas sucked. He was glad it was over. It just wasn't Christmas without Dad around, anyway. They hadn't even invited all the relatives over this year. And they did that every year. Never fail. Except for this time.

Tim kicked an unopened present near the foot of his bed and it skidded across the carpet. "Where the hell are you, Dad?"

He heard his sister moving around in her room. "Hey, Claire, come here!"

"What for?" she hollered.

"Because I said so." He heard a long, drawn out sigh, then the shuffling of little feet coming through the connecting bathroom. "What are you doing?"

"Reading a book."

"Where's Mom? What's she doing?"

Claire shrugged her tiny shoulders and turned to leave.

"Wait a minute."

Claire was looking at her brother, eyes full of innocence. "What?"

"What's with that drawing you made for Mom?" Tim climbed off the bed and looked down at his little sister.

Claire shrugged once more. Tim found her exasperating at times.

"I just made it," she said. She ran a hand through her hair.

"But why? Tell me about it. I mean, what's it supposed to be?"

"I told you, it's Daddy and the angels and the devil."

"In an alien world?"

"That's right, Tim."

He gave this some thought. "So what about that black knight dude? What's he supposed to be?"

Claire's eyes darkened. "That's the devil," she whispered. "He's bad."

Tim tossed his pillow at her. "You're looney, you know that?"

Claire shrugged yet again. Tim felt like shouting at her to knock it off. His sister started to leave but Tim held her back. "And you get to this alien world by traveling under the ocean?"

"That's right."

"Claire," said Tim, "how do you know this?" He held her shoulders to keep her from shrugging for the umpteenth billionth time.

"I just know." She broke free of her brother. "I'm tired. I'm going to bed now. 'Night."

Tim followed his young sister to her room and tucked her into the covers. This was Mom's job, but she wasn't here. He patted Claire's forehead. "Goodnight, Claire."

"Goodnight, Tim." She rolled onto her side. "And don't worry. The Devil isn't going to get Daddy."

"Are you sure?" whispered Tim.

Claire sat back up and crossed her legs. "Yep, I'm gonna draw another picture. Daddy's gonna destroy the Devil."

Tim smiled. "Right now you should get some sleep."

"Okay." Claire flopped back down on the mattress. "I'll work on it tomorrow."

"You do that," said Tim, softly, as he turned out the light and closed her door.

With alacrity, George jumped aboard the lead ship, whose name was Land Follower. He'd grown tired of sitting around Ryaii, waiting for something to happen; knowing that it must and that he'd might as well get it over with. Either that or wake up and go back to sleep.

Hello, Dr. Grossman. Are you out there?

He ran an admiring hand along the highly polished rail. "What are these ships made of anyway?"

"Sedoc," replied Ungris, who stood at George's side, a duffel bag over his shoulder. "The finest wood available. Costly as hell."

George's fingers stroked the rail. "It almost feels alive."

"It is alive."

"What?" George pulled his fingers back like they'd been burned.

"Sedoc can be cut and fashioned if you are careful and respectful. Treat her well and she'll treat you well. But abuse her and—" Ungris shrugged the duffel off his shoulder.

"And what?"

"And down you'll go." Ungris turned and spat over the side.

"You mean sink? You're saying if you don't treat this sedoc respectfully that this entire ship could sink? This entire fleet?"

Ungris was nodding along with every word. "That's right."

"That's not right," said George. "That's nonsense."

Ungris picked up his bag and headed belowdecks. "Suit yourself. I'm going to claim a bunk."

As Ungris sank from sight, George muttered. "Nonsense. Ungris is a fool. Half the things he says and does are crazy. Still . . ."

George patted the rail tenderly. He twisted his head to be certain no one was watching. "Good ship," he said, giving her a another gentle pat. "Good ship."

George stepped away from the rail and went in search of Cleea. Talking to boats! Dear God, if Elaine and Doc Grossman could seen him now they'd really think he'd gone off the deep end. And the trouble was, they'd be right.

He found Cleea belowdecks in the chartroom bent over a stretched out map which she studied intensely. "Which way to Oz?"

Cleea looked up, puzzled.

"Oz, you know. Dorothy, Toto. . ."

Cleea was staring at him.

"The Tin Man?"

"I do not understand, George. Who is this Tin Man? A friend of yours?"

"No, he's—Never mind." He looked at the map, an ink-drawn affair of mountains and incomprehensible squiggles. "So, exactly where are we headed?"

Cleea smiled. "That I can answer." She dropped her finger to the map. "We are here, Ryaii."

George nodded.

"We go to the Forest of Nightfall." She moved her finger in an upward arc to a bulging continent. "Here. Then we leave our ships and take to the Rive." She looked George in the eye. "If this meets your approval?"

"What?" Here we go again, thought George. The angel wanted his opinion. Either she was crazier than he was or they just weren't making angels like they used to. "Sure, whatever. I mean, that sounds fine. Excellent."

"Thank you."

"So, how soon before we shove off?"

Cleea closed her eyes for a moment. When she reopened them, she said, "We are already underway."

"We are? I don't feel anything. I mean, it doesn't even feel like we're moving."

Cleea was smiling. "Give it time."

"What do you mean?"

"The sea will show herself to us. I fear we will feel her agony."

George didn't know what the angel meant, but it didn't bode well no matter what. He opened a portal and looked out. Sure enough, the dock was a thousand meters away and shrinking fast. The sky was a bluish-purple. No clouds, no Mister Sun.

"Tell me, Cleea," George said, still looking out the tiny circle, "where is the sun?"

"Why do you ask, George? Did you lose it?"

For one long moment, George considered throwing himself out the window and into the sea. Maybe he'd give this drowning thing a second chance. The infuriating angel had sounded so serious in her response that he couldn't be angry with her, only with himself. He crossed his arms over his chest and determined not to surrender.

Besides, the stinking portal was far too small for him to pass through. Nothing larger than a suicidal imp would fit through one of those tiny things.

He worked his way deeper belowdecks. The heavy scent of saltwater and exotic foods filled the dark, low hallway. Where had Ungris gone? The hall branched off in two directions. The galley was to his left.

George was about to shout out Ungris's name when a pair of swinging doors opened and a gray-skinned Llorri stepped into the hall, doubled over because he was too tall to stand upright. It looked like the same one that had tried to kill Ungris and him in Thudor's lair. The Llorri stared at his hands, clenching and unclenching them slowly.

George held his breath. The monster was facing the other way and hadn't yet spotted him. George pushed his back against the wall as if he might blend in with the wood, yet knowing he would not. If the Llorri looked in his direction, he was a goner.

The Llorri scratched the top of his skull then lumbered off to the right, never once looking back. He went through an open doorway several doors up.

George, hand on his dagger, tiptoed after it. Not a sound came from the dimly lit cabin. George decided to risk a peek. After all, if there was one of those unkillable monsters aboard, Cleea and the others needed to know.

George bent low and quietly pushed his head around the doorframe. The giant had Ungris in his arms and was squeezing him slowly to death. George swallowed hard and made up his mind in a flash. After all, even if it meant losing his life, Ungris had taken just the same gamble for his sake. The least he could do was to die trying to save his friend.

George backed against the far wall of the narrow hall, giving himself some extra room for a running jump.

And jump he did. He hurled himself through the air and came down on the giant's back. The thing grunted and twisted his head. George pounded on the creature's muscle-knotted shoulders.

"George!" hollered Ungris. The Llorri's arms fell open and Ungris tumbled to the ground, bumping the back of his skull against a low wooden cot. "What the hell are you doing?"

"Run!" cried George. "Get the others!"

The giant's puzzled eyes stared into George's. He looked more curious than afraid. And George couldn't understand why Ungris was just lying there. Why wasn't the dolt getting up and running for assistance? His injuries couldn't be that serious. "What are you doing? Are you dazed? Get up!"

A smile broke out on Ungris' face. The smile turned into a raucous laugh. Ungris slapped his knees and pulled himself up onto the cot.

A giant arm came around and plucked George off by the shirt. The Llorri held George before him in his extended arm and looked him over.

"George," said Ungris, between gulps of air, "I'd like you to meet my friend, Potaster."

"Potaster," said Ungris with a wave of his hand, "this is the mighty George."

Potaster lowered George so that his feet touched the ground. George yanked himself free of the Llorri.

George looked up at the bald, craggy-headed giant. "Your friend?"

Potaster held out a hand the size of a catcher's mitt. It swallowed George's own like lunch.

"Potaster is on our side, George," said Ungris.

"He's one of the Llorri, isn't he?"

"I am," replied the giant with a gravel-laced voice that came from the depths of his throat. "And I am not."

George was looking at Ungris for answers.

"He fights for Cloudja. He has sworn his allegiance to us."

George pulled his hand free of Potaster's grip. "Sorry about all that."

The giant grinned. "It was nothing."

George frowned. *Nothing* was probably right. He had a suspicion that the giant had barely felt his mighty blows. Whereas George's hands throbbed and would likely be throbbing and bruised for days to come. Pounding on the Llorri had been like smashing his fists against a granite boulder.

Over hefty mugs of thick brown beer that smelled of strong clover honey, George heard the tale of Potaster. The Llorri, he learned, were of an ancient race of giants. Their home was far to the south in a region of tall mountains bordering thrashing seas.

The giants carved cities out of the bare rock and thrived for many ages. But theirs was a hard life and slowly the numbers of the Llorri dwindled. Agents of Thudor came and plied the Llorri with their own tales of riches to be easily made and lives more fruitful and bountiful. 'Why work the land so hard when one can take what one needs?' asked these base villains.

Slowly, many of the Llorri were swayed by these arguments buried in layers of false promises. Until the City of

Llovinda, their capital, had fallen completely under Thudor's spell.

"I believe," said Potaster, rather somberly, "that this is truly a spell." He shook his mighty head. "Lord Hiel has much power. It is my belief that he has transferred some such powers to Thudor and, thus, allowed him to conquer my people without so much as a fist raised in defiance." The giant coughed.

"And yet you have not succumbed?" questioned George, feeling the buzz of the beer as it coursed through his veins. "Why?"

Potaster shrugged. "I have always been different. An outsider. Perhaps Thudor's black magic was unable to affect me."

Ungris slapped Potaster across the back. "Pot's a tough old bird."

The Llorri grinned.

"You don't look so old," commented George.

"Tell George how old you are," urged Ungris.

"Eleven-hundred and twenty-one years."

George found himself searching Potaster's face, scanning the deep gray lines of his flesh. Wondering if what the Llorri said was true and, if so, how this could be. What would it be like to live so long?

"I have seen much," said Potaster softly, as if answering George's unspoken questions.

"And you'll see much more." Ungris rose and pulled the half-empty keg of beer from the bureau. "We all shall."

With that, he refilled their glasses. George thought about Ungris' words. He'd already seen more than he could have imagined. What more he would see, he could not even begin to dream of.

What would become of him? Of them all?

—22—

Three days passed and the dome of a distant continent turned from a gray blur to black and then to green.

Despite Cleea's warning, the seas had remained calm and, all in all, the trip had been pleasant enough. George had always wanted a boat and Land Follower was as fine as they come. When he got home he was going to get a boat for sure.

And it beat a turtle shell any day.

The ships were anchored several hundred meters from shore. From here, the canoes, filled with supplies, were lowered over the sides.

George helped Ungris with a large barrel which he was attempting to manhandle to the ship's side. "What have you got in there?"

"Brosia," grunted Ungris.

"That's a lot of brosia."

"The Rive Osfall is a lot of river." Ungris' chest heaved

up and down. The barrel rested on the rail. The two men gripped it unsteadily.

"It'll never fit in one of the canoes." The canoes were a good ten meters long and two wide, but they were, as far as George could see, quite full already. Especially when one figured in that each row had to seat two, possibly three, persons.

"Don't have to." Ungris suddenly pushed and the barrel hung in the air for a moment then plunged into the sea with a splash.

"What the—"

Ungris slapped George on the shoulder. "Don't you worry. In about half an hour, she'll wash ashore."

George watched as the barrel sloshed back and forth in the moving waters. At first, he feared Ungris had miscalculated and the brew would soon drift out to sea, but before long, the wooden barrel was making slow but steady progress towards shore.

What Ungris expected to do with it once it reached shore was another question. Was Ungris determined to carry the thing around on his back?

George joined Cleea and about two dozen others in one canoe. Sharan and Ungris were in another. Canoes from other ships had already reached the shore and soon their small party joined them. The sand was fine with a layer of heavier gray and black pebbles sprinkled over the top like seasoning.

"It's nearly dark. We'll camp here this night," said Cleea,

dropping her pack. The Rive Osfall is a day's journey to the north. We start in the morning." She turned to Sharan. "Have everyone ready to move at sunrise."

"Yes, Cleea." Sharan bowed and headed off to pass on Cleea's orders.

George wandered up the beach to the edge of the wood. The call of the rich green canopy beckoned. He heard exotic sounds, like monkeys and parrots.

"I would not wander too far, George."

He turned. It was Cleea. "Why not? Is the forest dangerous?"

"There is danger in everything," said Cleea, with little emotion. "Even dreams."

George wondered if Cleea knew just what sort of dreams he'd been having. For they were indeed dangerous, dangerous and deadly. "Tell me, Cleea, do you ever think of dying?"

Cleea smiled. "Each day, there is a choice, we either live or we die." She looked up at the sky. "When we live, we must embrace life." She caught George's eyes. "If the choice is death, we must embrace this also."

"Easier said than done," replied George.

"Isn't everything?" There wasn't a trace of sarcasm in her voice. "Come, George. There is little time."

Well, thought George, as he followed his angel back to camp. There was little time. That was something. All he'd ever heard her say before was that there was no time.

Maybe they were making progress.

They slept outdoors on blankets stretched out in the sand. There were no stars. George didn't bother asking why. Tiny insects seemed to insinuate themselves under his skin and George spent the night scratching at them.

Oddly enough, he found himself missing the blue fountain. The susurrus of its flowing waters, its whisper in his ears had soothed him, made him feel less out-of-sorts, less homesick. Funny, he never thought he'd feel homesick—miss his old life. After all, what was there to miss? A business that he loathed?

Sometimes he just wanted to sell everything and take the wife and kids off to Idaho or somewhere equally remote. Live in a cabin in the woods, read great books of the past. Watch the children grow.

He scratched some more. They'd need some bug spray in Idaho.

When he woke in the morning, efforts were already underway to march. George grabbed a quick cold breakfast of cereal and juice that was orange in color but tasted more like strawberry. Ungris had called it gualac berry.

The troop's supplies had been distributed among them all and the canoes were to be carried several kilometers through the woods. Sharan explained that the waters where the Rive Osfall emptied into the sea were too rough and rock-filled to attempt in the canoes and, thus, they would have to be hauled overland until they reached quieter waters.

Claire sat at her student desk, back straight as a washboard, diligently applying colored pencil to drawing paper. She could hear the muffled sounds of Gameboy coming from Tim's room.

Claire hadn't seen her mother all morning. Tim said she was still in bed. She wasn't even going to the office and she always went to the office—went early and stayed late. Often, Mother came home from the office only to plop herself down at the computer in the home office and work some more. Claire wondered if this was the Devil's fault, too.

Claire drew several lines that sliced through the air and formed the beginnings of a star, then stopped, displeased with her work. "This is going to be harder than I thought," she groused aloud. "How is Daddy going to defeat the Devil?"

She turned the paper over and started again. But this picture looked even worse and she tossed it in the wastebasket.

Claire leaned back, closed her eyes and let her mind empty. Somewhere inside herself was the answer.

She just knew it.

—23—

The first thing that Rabo did was throw up.

At least he'd had the presence of mind to do it over the side of the boat.

The white-suited guy was laughing. He stopped when Rabo turned, glaring in his direction.

"I am sorry," said Gason, his eyes wrinkling at the corners. "I mean you no offense."

Rabo wiped the spittle from his face with the back of his sleeve. "None taken, I suppose." He glanced at Quill. Jesus, she looked catatonic. "So where are we exactly? And who are you guys supposed to be? The Coast Guard?"

"They're Uppers," said Quill. She'd said 'uppers' like it was a curse or the impetus of their doom.

Rabo eyed the man and woman warily. His hands ready to fight—why or what he didn't know.

Gason passed a tender eye over Quill. "Do we look like

Uppers?" He tugged at his white suit. "Do we dress in their fashion?"

His long arms spread wide. "Does this look like one of their great yachts that ride above the sea?"

Quill made no reply.

Rabo went to her side and squatted beside her on the deck. "He's right, Quill," he said softly. "I mean, they don't look like they're rich."

The man's suit was plain and simple; and the woman, Cloudja, wore a white gown that ended above her well-turned ankles. But the gown also was plain and simply cut.

Without looking Rabo in the eye, Quill responded, "They don't look like Lowers either."

Rabo chewed on this opinion. No, they did not. Most certainly did not. "Well, whatever they are, they've saved us."

Now she was looking into his eyes, boring into them like her own hollow eyes had spouted stainless steel drill bits. "Being saved requires something to be saved from, does it not? Being saved just-just to go back there. . .below."

She hugged herself, shivering. "That's not being saved. That's not being saved at all. If they wanted to save us, they should have killed us. The only salvation from a life in Hell is death." Her body convulsed.

Rabo snatched a nearby scratchy brown blanket and drew it over her shoulders.

"Then I would thank them,"spat Quill.

Rabo rose. He stood before the man. "She's got a point, you know."

Gason nodded, then looked over Rabo's shoulder towards the woman. "We've no intention of returning you back there. Not after all the trouble we've had getting you here."

Rabo was taken aback. All the trouble they'd had getting them here? What on earth was that supposed to mean?

"What about João?" Quill said dully.

"Yes," Rabo said, "there was another person with us."

Cloudja spoke up. "Yes, the boy. We seek him yet."

Gason turned his back on Rabo and the girl and took the helm with large, strong and able hands. "And we'll find him. The gills with which the Lowers were genetically altered are base and cannot sustain life in the sea indefinitely. He must surface."

"Or die," added Quill.

"Isn't there anything more you can do?" Rabo asked of Gason.

"We listen to the sea." He glanced at Cloudja.

Cloudja leaned over the rail, dipped her arm, nearly to her elbow, into the sea as if testing the waters. She straightened and pointed her dripping hand. "João has gone in that direction." She was aiming toward the southeast.

Gason turned the bobbing boat and followed the line she'd drawn.

Cloudja knelt beside Quill and took the girl's limp wrist in her hand. "You are malnourished. There is food below. Fruit and nuts. And fresh water. I will bring it."

"So," said Rabo, standing alongside Gason, who towered

over him by more than a head, "if you aren't Uppers and you aren't Lowers, what are you?"

"I am Gason."

"You said that. Got anything else?"

Gason smiled. His strong fingers clenched the wheel and turned it slightly to the right. "I am the companion of Cloudja."

"You call that some kind of answer? Who are you? Where are you from? What are you doing out here, in the middle of the stinking ocean?"

"Hiel has placed his hand across Time. He seeks to hold Cloudja prisoner here." One of Gason's hands lifted from the wheel and swept the air as if clearing it of dust. "In this place."

Rabo studied the white-gowned woman with the diamonds in her hair. "So just who is this Cloudja and why would this Hiel guy want to make her prisoner? And who is he anyway?"

"Hiel," said Gason soberly, "is the Lord of the Deep Refuge. My lady, High Queen Cloudja, is Guardian of the Eye. Hiel seeks to destroy the Eye or, at the least, subvert it to his malevolent uses."

If Rabo's eyebrows had ridden up any higher, they'd have been floating in space. "Man, you sound like a comic book. This can't be real."

Gason shrugged his wide shoulders. "As you wish."

"As I—" There was a tumultuous swelling on the starboard side. Water and air burst over the surface like a giant bubble. The boat tipped precariously to port. Cloudja clung to Quill and both slid across the deck, slamming heavily into the opposite side.

After a struggle, Gason settled the boat.

Rabo was sweating, though he'd done nothing except strive to maintain his balance at best and keep from falling overboard at least. He wasn't used to boats. Never been on one in his life. Wished he was not on one now. "What on earth was that?"

Quill spoke up. "A burst wall. Many Lowers will have died." Cloudja thrust a purple chunk of peeled fruit in Quill's face. She eyed it warily, then wolfed it hungrily.

Quill eyed the remaining food in Cloudja's hands with equal hunger. Cloudja smiled and handed it over. Quill's jaw muscles worked quickly. Her gaunt cheeks filled with food. Quill was unable to swallow it all quickly enough, so she hoarded it in her mouth like a squirrel. Perhaps fearful that winter would suddenly come and leave her starving once more, or that the Cloudja would snatch it away, leaving her only her hunger.

When you're poor no one can take that away from you. They can take much, but they cannot take your hunger.

"Is it true that's what happened? There was an accident below?" Rabo's hands gripped the boat. Suddenly floating on this wretched little vessel in the middle of the uncaring ocean seemed like a little bit of paradise compared to being trapped in the world below.

"Those below are not given the best quality materials."

Gason swung the wheel. "Or food. These things are saved for those up here."

"I still don't understand how you and Cloudja fit into all this."

"We are trapped in this place and time by Hiel."

"Why? What have you done to him?"

Gason smiled. "It is not what we do, it is what we prevent."

Rabo looked confused.

"You see, Hiel believes that with Cloudja out of the way he can subvert the Eye and wrest control of the world."

"This world?"

"All the worlds that represent this world."

"My world?"

"You are a part of this world."

Rabo laughed. "I don't think so." He looked across the sea towards the pale outline of the shore. "I mean, I barely recognize this place. It looks sort of like my home. But changed."

Gason spoke matter-of-factly. "You come from another time. An earlier time."

"An-an earlier time?"

Gason had his back to the young man and his hair fluttered in the wind. "A thousand years. Eleven hundred and three, to be exact."

Rabo stepped backward, his mind and legs reeling.

—24—

The forest turned to jungle and they trudged through it.

Ungris was in foul spirits. Cleea had forced him to leave behind his brosia—despite his pleas and argument of all the trouble he'd gone to hauling it halfway across the world—but not before he'd filled several flasks which he'd placed in his pack. He'd also begged and cajoled several of the others, including George, to do the same on his behalf.

George's pack dug into his shoulders. His feet sunk in the soft earth. Humid air filled his lungs. Yet the scent of life was everywhere; in every insect that buzzed around his dripping face, in every plant that whipped his legs and arms.

George smiled.

He was alive.

They stopped at the shore of a green lake and, after much discussion, lowered the canoes. Impossibly, the strokes of their paddles made not the slightest waves in the water.

Everyone remained silent. Not even the normally garrulous Ungris felt like speaking, while Potaster hung his head, chin against his chest, as if troubled or saddened by some pain unspoken.

George studied the pale blue sky. Not a single cloud floated overhead. Not a single bird scooted past. Not a solitary fish disturbed the still waters.

He was relieved to reach the other side and solid ground once more. The lake had made him uneasy. He almost felt as though it had been calling him. But that was crazy.

Wasn't it?

They hefted the canoes back onto their shoulders and marched into the high-canopied forest. It seemed to George much like the Amazonian rain forests which he only knew from books. One of those places he always wanted to visit and never had.

Maybe never would. . .

He caught up to Cleea towards the fore of the troop. "Is it really worth lugging all these canoes along with us?"

"We shall need them soon enough. We will reach the Rive Osfall before night."

George gaped at the giant trees overhead. "So this is the Forest of Nightfall?"

Cleea nodded. "We are safe enough here. Our troubles shall begin when we enter the river."

"What is it? Strong currents? Rapids?" George swatted some invisible insect that seemed to be nipping at his ears.

"Yes," said Cleea after a moment. "But that is nothing we

cannot handle. The Rive Osfall is exposed. The Lord of the Deep and Thudor will expect us there. Though their power is limited on the water because of the Rive Osfall's own magic, they will try to destroy us."

She'd said this way too matter-of-factly for George's taste.

"Then why enter it at all? Isn't there some other way to reach this Orexis?" Not that he was in any hurry himself to reach it or Thudor's armies.

Cleea paused in her tracks. "There is the Hoven Canyon. To the east." She pointed into the woods to her right. "It is deep with a well-worn trail."

"Sounds good to me."

Cleea turned and faced him. "It is as you wish, George."

George hesitated. She'd march them all straight into the ocean if he so much as suggested it. "Is there any particular problem with going through this Hoven Canyon?"

She shrugged, took a sip of water from her sac before speaking. "There is danger everywhere."

"Such as?"

"I cannot say. None of our scouts have ever returned from within Hoven Canyon to speak of such."

George's eyebrows shot up. That was enough information for him. He took Cleea's hand. "No sense changing course now."

At her desk, Claire yawned. She had been thinking and thinking and drawing and drawing and nothing, nothing seemed right somehow. She pressed her eyes shut and rolled the blunted crayon around in her mouth.

She knew her father was out there. She knew that she could help him. If she could only catch up with him.

Claire pictured a brilliant orange ball in her mind's eye and absentmindedly her hand squeezed the image onto the crumpled, sweat-stained paper on her desk.

George coughed, struggling for breath. He smelled smoke. Something was pulling at him. He opened his eyes to find the giant Llorri, Potaster, grabbing at him. George's face turned to fright before he remembered that Ungris had insisted the Llorri was their friend.

"What's wrong?" grunted George, wearily. He hadn't had nearly enough rest and his muscles ached terribly.

"We are under attack. Look!" The giant stepped out of George's face.

George sat up. Brown smoke billowed from around the edges of the camp. The canoes were on fire and everyone was rushing around trying to put out the flames. He jumped to his feet. "Who is it? What is it?"

There was bedlam in all directions. Some odd looking brutes, with fat, hairy bellies and slings in their long crooked arms were hurtling fiery missiles in all directions. The stench of burning wood and burning flesh weighed heavy on the air.

"Creatures of the Emnon. They live under the earth and feed of the fires of Mont Vastnon, a volcano deep in the bowels of the Centron Plains. They are allies of Thudor. He has promised them a place in the New Order, no doubt, in exchange for doing his bidding."

A flaming ball of fire, like a fist-sized meteorite, shot between George and Potaster. "They've destroyed the craft. They aim to destroy us next, George." The Llorri pushed George behind an outcropping of rock. "Stay here."

George made to protest but he was no match for the Llorri who tossed him behind the rocks like he was no more than a small child. A small and helpless child.

George pressed up to the cold rock listening to the sounds of rabid battle, wishing he could help and not knowing how he might. As he raised his head to survey the fight's progress, a searing pain pierced his back. He cried out and turned. One of the Emnon stood a mere meter away, an ugly, sharp-toothed grin upon its black, oval face.

The Emnon's grin widened as he drew another flaming ball from a seemingly endless supply in the pouch slung over his shoulder. He curled the fiery ball in his hand, bouncing it lightly in his palm. "Georgesh," he said with a slur, bringing his arm back in a threatening posture, "thish ish for shou."

So this is how it ends, thought George. This is what it feels like to die. Was this truly his death? Or was this all some fever-induced fantasy? Was he lying in some hospital ward in South Florida, dying in some much more mundane fashion?

No matter.

George gazed steadily at this creature who would murder him and held his gaze as the thick arm drew back and shot forward. The burning rock came towards him in slow motion. At the last second, even as he felt the heat on his cheeks and neck, George flinched.

The rock skated across the top of his skull and he felt nothing more.

Claire drew her work-in-progress from the top drawer of her desk, chewed on her lip some, then set to work. Usually it was easy to draw. She'd just start moving her crayon or a colored pencil around on the paper and see what grew. But this was different.

This took lots of concentration. She paused, looking at the clumsy green lines she had drawn. She still wasn't satisfied. She lifted the paper to the window, letting the morning's light filter through.

Claire tilted the paper from side to side. Somewhere in there was the picture she was trying to make. She knew it existed. Just like she knew where Daddy was and what he was doing.

She picked up a black crayon and pushed it forcefully along the paper. All her emotions ran through, from her brain, curving through her shoulder, running down her arm like liquid flames rising up in her fingers and finally being absorbed into the waxy crayon.

"Hey, Claire!"

There was an impatient knock on her bedroom door. That would be Timmy.

"Come on, Claire." He pushed open the door, stepped over her shoes and yesterday's clothes which lay spread out over the carpet and turned her around as she sat in her chair.

"Come on, already. Lunch is waiting."

Lunch? Was it that late? It felt like she'd only just eaten breakfast. "I'm coming."

"Hey, what happened to you?"

"What do you mean?"

"You're all sweaty."

Claire looked at her arms. They glistened. Her shirt was soaked through. Drops of sweat fell from her brow to the ground. "I don't know."

"What have you got there?" Tim eyed her rolled up paper warily, wondering what the goofy kid was up to now.

"Nothing." She wormed her way past him and walked straight to the kitchen. She paused in front of the refrigerator. It was a veritable wall of magnets holding up family photos and drawings as well as a grocery list which hadn't been updated since—since their father had disappeared.

Claire pulled down a couple of school drawings, unrolled her paper and hung it up. Then she reached in her pant pocket and withdrew a folded piece of lined white paper. She unfolded the paper carefully and stuck it up with a magnet, too.

Without another word, let alone an explanation, she plopped herself down on her chair at the table and attacked her lunch.

Tim studied the drawing for a moment, uncertain what it was exactly and what to make of it. Then he turned his attention to her letter. He couldn't believe it.

Dear Daddy,

This is Claire. I want you to know that I know where you are and why you are gone and what you are doing. I am doing all I can to help. I am trying real hard. I drew another picture. I hope it helps. I'm not very good drawing stuff. If there is anything you need, please let me know and I will try to get it to you. And please, be careful, Daddy. You are in danger, but I know you'll be all right. We all love you and miss you.

Love, Claire

Tim realized he had been holding his breath. Slowly, he inhaled. He looked over his shoulder at his little sister. She was sitting there eating her perfectly normal peanut butter and jelly like everything else was perfectly normal, too.

Like she was perfectly normal!

Man, something weird was going on.

He thought about removing the letter before Mom saw it. She might flip her lid. Mom might very well have a fit and start yelling at the both of them.

But something impalpable kept him from touching Claire's message. Maybe he didn't want to get Claire mad at him. Or maybe he was afraid that if he tore it up or even took it down Dad would be hurt.

But that was just plain crazy. Wasn't it?

Tim sat down across the table from Claire, watching her eat, shoving his potato chips around and around on his plate.

Since Dad had gone, things had gotten weird. Mom and Claire were acting nutty.

Was he getting crazy, too?

The world seemed to be falling apart around him. Claire, who was a bitty nutty to begin with, had withdrawn even further into her own little world—a world that Tim couldn't begin to see or comprehend.

Mom was going to pieces. Oh, some days she looked pretty normal. But Tim could tell she was having a hard time keeping things together. Tough as nails, SuperBusinessWoman Mom—she was losing it.

She'd needed Dad more than he would have thought, more than she'd probably expected herself.

For the umpteenth time since he'd disappeared, Tim wondered where his father was and if he was still alive. For the umpteenth time since seeing Claire's note to Dad, Tim opened his mouth to ask her what it was supposed to mean—just how she expected Dad to see it, if she did.

Did she think he was living in the walls, sneaking out at night to raid the refrigerator?

He stuck a chip in his mouth instead. It went in wrong and the sharp, salty edges cut into the roof of his mouth. He chewed up the pieces and washed down the remains with a glass of cold milk. He wiped his lips with the back of his arm. "I think I'll take a drive after lunch. You want to come?"

"No, thanks." Claire rose. She carried her lunch dishes to the sink and rinsed them off.

"Why not?"

"I have some stuff to do." Claire pulled a cookie from the cookie jar.

"You'll have to stay home with Mom." Their mother was in the study, working. She wasn't much company these days.

"That's okay." Claire started down the hall, then stopped. "You won't find him, you know."

Tim looked startled. "Who?"

"Daddy." Claire went away.

Tim stared at the space where she'd been. How had she known that he was intending to look for their father?

–25–

A yellow-green, saw-edged fern cut across George's cheek. He cursed and thrust it away. The jungle was closing in on their small troop. Spirits were low. There was little talk and much grumbling.

George plodded on.

But something more was wrong. George could feel it. Since coming to this world he'd developed senses far greater than he had ever possessed at home. The jungle seemed now to be holding its breath. The insects and birds shied away and a low, sick noise took their place.

"George?"

"Huh?" He looked up, and realized that he was standing still.

"Is something wrong, George?" Cleea was a good ten meters ahead of him. Others were marching past him now as well.

"I'm not sure." He turned his head and took in a panoramic view of the dense junglescape. "Something isn't right."

Then again, nothing had seemed right since he'd woken after the battle with the Emnon. His scalp still caused him pain and he'd lost chunks of hair. He'd come to in time to find the battle over and the Emnon defeated. The one who had tried to kill George had been slain by Potaster. The Llorri had shown George the corpse as if it would please him.

It did not, though he didn't tell the giant this. After all, the big guy had meant well.

And now, with all but two of the canoes reduced to ashes by the Emnon, their little army had been forced to follow a trail through the Hoven Canyon. After all, the canoes had been their only means of transportation down the Rive Osfall.

This had probably been Lord Hiel's intention all along. Forcing them all, George included, to follow the course he dictated. A rage welled up inside whenever George contemplated this. The nightmarish battles between himself and Hiel grew stronger each night, so much so that he dreaded the inevitable collapse of sleep that must come each and every day.

In the meantime, the army's advance had been reduced to a cautious crawl. George hoped that this Thudor character didn't mind them arriving a little late.

George shook his head of doubts and fears. He repeated what he's said about something not feeling right. "I don't know what it is though."

Cleea nodded. "I feel it, too. But we must continue. There is no time." She held her fingers to her lips and whistled. A moment later, a distant, shrill reply came. That would be Sharan. It was the way that the two angels communicated with one another. "I do not like that we have no visual contact with the entire expedition. It leaves us more vulnerable to attack."

George agreed. "The sooner we get out of here the better." He resumed walking and forced himself to pick up the pace. He didn't know where he was going but he was in something of a hurry to get there. Besides, he'd seen enough John Wayne movies to know that they were vulnerable here.

The soft, flat ground grew harder underfoot and they began a long slope downward over a beige colored soil. A canyon of granite rose around them as they descended. It grew hotter. There was a sweetness to the air as if it had been laced with sugar.

The grumbling of the troop had stopped now. Eyes moved in every direction as if all feared an unseen and impending danger.

They appeared like small ghosts at first, growing and thickening in a matter of seconds. Their pasty skin and eyeless faces sent a wave of awe and fear up George's spine. There were hundreds of them and they appeared to come from the walls of the canyon itself.

They had naked pink bodies and were all fuzzy-featured. One appeared near George and reached out its hand. It lighted on George's arm, all clammy and cold. George recoiled and slid to his knees.

The creature reached for him and he jumped to his feet.

Gaping mouths, from which no light escaped, opened and closed with horrible sucking sounds. Two more creatures, rasping wickedly, grabbed George's arm and he struggled to remove himself from their bone-crushing grips. Their flesh felt like plastic, bloodless putty.

The bloodless creatures rained down on the troop. Weapons were drawn and the tiny army fought valiantly against the onslaught but their weapons seemed ineffectual against such bewildering and inhuman brutes.

George heard whistling in every direction as he slashed at their arms with his blade. The creatures' mouths stretched in soundless howls that George could only imagine. His dagger sliced through their hands and forearms like it was cookie dough. A hand grabbed George by the collar and pulled him back.

George swung around, ready to strike. "Ungris!"

"Hurry, George!" hollered his liberator. "Ahead!"

Ungris pushed George forward. He stumbled over loose rock. His knife was wrapped in his hand and he held it in front of him. More creatures leapt from the cliff face. George heard screaming, saw several of his party fall. One fellow, a scruffy bearded man named Mundrian who had been a shipmate of George's, collapsed lifelessly to the ground as several of the exotic creatures pummeled his body.

"Come on, George!" urged Ungris. "What are you waiting

for?" He tugged George's shirt. "Do something! We'll all die!"

George stared helplessly at the carnage forming around them. What was he supposed to do?

What the hell was he supposed to do?

—26—

George threw Ungris off him. "I want to go home!" he shouted. "Leave me alone."

Ungris fell to the ground and scrambled to his feet.

"I want to go home!"

George closed his eyes and squeezed hard. The world shimmered. He felt himself unsteady on his feet as if a wave had suddenly caught him and was tossing him about like nothing more than a toy boat.

He caught a vision of his wife, Elaine, in her blue dress, the one she always wore when she was depressed or in a funk. She was at her desk. Doing nothing. Her fingers still. Her eyes vacant, red, swollen and staring at nothing.

Claire was on her bed, drawing. Tim was racing towards him, recklessly steering the Volvo. About to run him down?

Something hard struck George on the back. He thrust out his arms, afraid he'd fall. His eyes popped open automatically.

Cleea was hugging him. She was smiling.

"Thank you, George." She hugged him once more, so hard he was certain he'd busted a couple of ribs. Then she released him.

He frowned. "For what?"

"For saving us."

Ungris, off to one side, spat. "Could have done it a lot sooner. Saved us a lot of death." He let out a loud breath. "Some of those folks were my friends."

George looked at the quiet carnage. The creatures lay still in heaps on the ground, as if they'd simply run down, out of steam or batteries or bug juice or what ever the hell it was that they ran on. Maybe they were wind-up toys. Who knew? Not George.

But those weren't the dead Ungris alluded to. Members of the expedition gathered the corpses of their own army. George sat on the ground, feeling the coolness of the rock creep up into his bones. Cleea kept him company. Though she said nothing.

After some time had passed, Sharan approached and squatted on her haunches. "We've lost many."

"How many?" asked Cleea.

"More than ninety."

Cleea blinked and sighed. "At this rate, we'll barely have an army left when we reach Orexis."

"Thudor will make an easy meal of us," Ungris predicted.

Sharan told him to keep his spirits up. "Courage is everything," she said. Cleea asked her if the dead had been attended to and Sharan said the ritual had begun.

Cleea rose and dusted herself off. "Will you join us, George?"

He shrugged and rose stiffly to his feet. Following Cleea and Sharan he found that most of the troop had formed into circles within circles around the bodies of their dead. Only a few dozen sentries remained outside of the circles, their eyes scanning the horizon and the sky above. George wondered what menace they watched for.

Cleea walked silently to the center, until she was amongst their fallen comrades. She held out her arms and began an elaborate invocation, her hands moving like hypnotic creatures with minds of their own. "Kuyavish, Atavish. Atavish, Kuyavish," she exclaimed, her voice somber, yet reverberating through the circles. " I. I know the power. I. I am the power. The power is mine. The power in mine." She paused and closed her eyes. "Be well."

"Be well," whispered the throng. George noticed they'd all closed their eyes and did the same. When he opened them, his dead comrades were gone. He gasped. Not a solitary trace remained. "What happened? Where did they go?" he whispered fervently to Sharan.

She cocked her head. "Who?"

"Who?! The dead, that's who!"

"They are dead, George. The dead are gone." She looked at him as if puzzled. "Are the dead not gone for you, George?"

"Of course they're gone," said George. "But they're not

gone gone." He pointed at the flattened earth where the bodies had lain only moments before. "Not like that."

Sharan still looked puzzled.

"We bury them," said George. "In the ground."

The woman's eyes grew wide. "Your ways are wondrous, George. Some day, perhaps you would honor me to teach them to me." With that, Sharan, turned on her heel and left to seek out Cleea.

If the gaping hole in George's mouth had opened any wider, he'd have fallen in.

That night, they slept in tents on the hard ground listening to the torrential rains that fell upon them. The wind howled relentlessly. George tossed and turned while his roommate, Ungris, snored loudly. How he could sleep through the racket George never knew. Cold water seeped into the unlined tents making a mess of his sleeping roll.

George pulled up the roll and used it for a seat, huddling in the corner of the tent away from the opening. He'd tied the flap firmly, but it looked like ready to burst against nature's onslaught. He took a light orb from his pack and dug around until he'd found the journal and pencil he knew he would find there.

He held the pencil over the paper, unsure what to say, what to write. Even what to think. . .

João's scrawny, limp figure was plucked from the sea by Gason as nimbly and easily as if he was landing an undersized perch. Rabo rushed to the boy and cupped his hand behind his neck. He coughed up seawater.

Gason leaned over and rubbed some smelly brown balm into the tiny gill slits behind João's ears. Quill was tucked into a corner of the boat, her knees to her chest. Withdrawn once again. She was in bad shape. Only her eyes showed any sign of life.

Then again, thought Rabo, João's eyes showed no signs of life at all. By comparison, Quill was not doing so poorly. "Can't you help him?"

Gason laid a hand over João's unmoving chest. Rabo anxiously watched.

Cloudja stood over him, the shadow of her figure crossing all three of them. She placed her hand on Rabo's shoulder. "He does all he can." She silently studied João's still form. "The boy will live." She let out a slow breath. "He must live."

Rabo wondered how she meant this. Was João's life important to her for some reason? If so, what?

Cloudja ordered João to be taken below. Rabo made to assist Gason but the big man lifted João in his arms and carried him belowdecks.

Rabo stared across the moving sea. The land had faded to a mere line on the horizon. He could no longer discern the familiar hump of Sugar Loaf. They'd drifted far. Far from home. Then again, if Gason was correct and wasn't deceiving him, he was farther from home than he would ever have dreamed possible.

He planted his fists on his hips and glared at Cloudja. Queen or not, he wanted answers and said so.

Cloudja smoothed down her gown. It was spotless and seemed impervious to moisture and dirt. Rabo wondered what miracle fabric it was made of. His mother would have loved it. She hated doing laundry.

"I am Cloudja. I have been imprisoned, trapped in this time and place by Lord Hiel. He seeks my undoing." Her slender arms swept through the air which grew chill around them. "He seeks the undoing of us all."

A shiver ran up Rabo's spine. Was it the air or the sense of foreboding that she exuded? He shrugged. He'd heard all this before. "What's this got to do with me? Why am I here? For that matter," he said, his voice rising, "how exactly did I get here?"

Cloudja's smile was simple and pure. "We willed you here. Our powers are not so diminished that we cannot wish. Did you not hear our call?"

Rabo's forehead crinkled like a rumpled paperbag. "Last thing I remember," he said, scratching his scalp, "is driving to work. On Avenue Rodrigues." His eyes closed and the scene came back, fuzzy yet sure. "There was a bus. I swerved. I-I think I hit the water." He opened his eyes and stared over the edge of the boat. "This water."

"And now you are here." Cloudja took Rabo's hand. Hers was warm, his own felt like it had been carved from a block of ice.

Yes, now I am here, thought Rabo. Wherever the hell *here*

was. Hell. The word and its meaning passed through him like a shock wave.

Maybe this was Hell.

He hadn't exactly been a saint the short twenty-three years of his life. Not that he thought he'd been bad enough to warrant an express trip to Hell. . .

Cloudja tugged his arm and he pulled out of his reverie. A faint scent of honeysuckle drifted from her locks. "You must hunger. The Lowers are never given enough."

Rabo nodded, noticing for the first time the rumbling in his belly. "Is that really Brazil out there? The way it's going to look in my future?"

Cloudja's eyes seemed to sadden. "It would appear so." She brightened. "Yet perhaps we can change this. Come, Rabo." She pulled him towards the galley.

Rabo stopped at the bulkhead. "What about her?" Quill sat silently against the side of the bobbing boat. Her hair clung to her face. She looked awfully pale despite very probably having finished the biggest meal of her life.

"Quill has had a difficult time. A hard life. Do not worry for her, Rabo. Quill's time will come. She will adjust." Cloudja swept her gown up around her ankles. "She awaits the drawing."

Rabo frowned. "The drawing?"

Cloudja nodded. "Children can do such marvelous things, can they not?"

Rabo followed this strange queen below in bumfuzzled silence.

George drew a picture of a turtle. It wasn't much of a turtle. But he wasn't much of an artist. He didn't know what to write, how to express what he felt and so he decided to compose a journal. Whether he or it would survive the days ahead was anyone's guess, including his.

He began with his descent into the ocean, a swirling memory of bright lights and cold water. Awakening in that cave-like chamber and meeting Cleea, his angel.

A boom like distant thunder shook the tent and George clutched his pencil tighter. He remembered that awful, black-skinned beast with the toadish eyes in the cavern so long ago.

George drew pictures of all the wondrous and unbelievable sights and creatures he had seen and met. Looking at the pictures he could only believe that he truly had lost his mind. What little of it there had been left to begin with.

A sad smile passed his countenance. He tried his hand at drawing likenesses of his family, Elaine, Tim and little Claire. He'd done a lousy job of it, but it warmed his heart to see even such primitive images of them nearby. He vowed to look at it every day and to add to his journal each evening.

A way of keeping in touch, he wondered, or of keeping a slender thread of his sanity?

A loud crack split the air once more and the tent burst open. "Cleea!"

She nodded. "Come, George!" She was dripping wet from head to toe and wiped beads of rain from her chin and eyes. "There is no time. We must go!" She looked at Ungris.

"Wake him and grab what you can." Cleea turned in the tent door. "But make haste!"

"But why? What's going on?" George groaned. Here we go again. It was no use. Cleea was gone, faded into the night. A fierce sound like the sky being torn in two pieces was all the impetus he needed to heed Cleea's words. He kicked the heavy-sleeping Ungris awake and yelled at him that they were leaving.

George recognized that sound. It was the same sound that had gotten Cleea in such a fright when they'd first met. What it was he didn't know. But if she was afraid of it, so was he.

Ungris rose, rubbed his eyes with his fists and started to complain. Yet another crackling boom shook the earth around them. "It's Himself!"

"What? Who?" George was busy thrusting his meager belongings into his backpack. "Help me with the tent."

Ungris shook his head madly and fled out-of-doors.

—27—

They ran through the rain. It pummeled them as fiercely as those strange creatures had only hours earlier. Forced to go forward in the dead of night, against what further nightmares George could only imagine.

Strange, inhuman sounds came from the walls of the canyon. George envisioned exotic, deadly monsters that would swoop down upon them all any moment and devour them whole. The rain created rock slides in the softer sections of the canyon. Jagged boulders and scree blocked their way, making the going slow and hard, forcing them to fight for every step and at every turn.

George lent a hand whenever he could; carrying supplies, dragging one of the two remaining canoes through the mud. Floadan, buck-toothed with oily black hair that hung over equally black eyes, a distant cousin of Ungris, held up the other end of the canoe.

Floadan was an ebullient man despite the fate before them and the odds against them. He had remained irrationally cheerful throughout the hard, quiet march.

George felt his sore bones building muscle and wondered to discover that his body contained more than layers of fat built from years of slouching behind his desk.

There was no sign of Ungris. He'd probably gone off ahead, scouting.

"Where has Ungris gone, Floadan?" George asked, his breath coming out in short, jagged puffs.

"My cousin has gone ahead with Sharan and a small band of listeners. The giant goes with them."

George nodded. He'd noticed that Potaster was missing as well. "Who are these listeners?"

"They are beings who possess the ability to hear what others can only see. They listen for signs of Thudor and his army."

"I don't get it," said George. "I thought we were going to meet this army of Thudor's at the Steppes of Orexis?"

"And so we shall, if Thudor does not change his plans."

The rains had stopped as suddenly as they'd come. Warm, humid wind swept into their faces.

"Where does Cloudja fit into all this?"

"The Queen?"

George nodded. "Is she with Thudor? If we win this battle," which he pretty much doubted, "will she be freed?"

Floadan waggled a thick eyebrow. "I cannot say. That is your domain, George, your responsibility." He lowered his head. "I am a mere balladeer. I sing songs of the past and, sometimes," he added, "with a twinkle in his eye, "of things that might be."

With that, Floadan tipped back his head and launched into a melody that was foreign and yet familiar all at once.

There is a land, a land far away
Near to our hearts, where we once lived
All our lives, all our children
All our future, together
So together we go forward, ahead
Searching for yesterday

Marching silently on, George, oddly, felt that he understood Floadan's song. Where was his yesterday? Was it behind him? Would he regain what he'd lost?

Those fragile, ephemeral images of Elaine, Tim and Claire that he'd seen in the Eye of the World. . .Looking up at them, George had felt that he might have reached out his hand and touched them, built a link between himself and his family. . .a link that might have taken him home.

If that monster, Hiel, hadn't spoilt it. George's jaw tightened and he squeezed his hands into hard fists. Damn that Hiel. Damn him to Hell. . .

"Get your stinking hands off me!" João punched Gason hard, right in the middle of his chin.

The blow glanced off Gason's unflappable face. He

turned his back on the boy and lumbered up the steep steps.

João glared at his retreating backside. "I hate that guy."

Rabo, sitting on a narrow bunk that hung from thick chains anchored in the wall, his legs dangling over the side, looked amused. "That's no reason to hit him. He's only trying to help."

João sourly studied his throbbing hand. He wasn't about to admit it, let alone to this weird Rabo character, but he regretted his actions. The big guy had only been trying to help. Probably. "Still, I don't trust him."

Rabo fell back against his pillow. "You don't trust anybody."

"That's right." There was a hard edge to the boy's voice. "I don't. You can't if you want to survive in my world."

Rabo propped up his head. "We're not in your world, João. We're not even in my world. No," he said, punching the feathers in his pillow, enjoying the softness of the blows, "you're a Lower. We're here," he waved his hands, "with the Uppers. Floating on a tub in the middle of the stinking ocean."

His nostrils involuntarily flared. It did stink, too. Cloudja had explained that the seas had become polluted to the point that they were nearly dead. The oceans had become almost unable to support life of any kind. What little did survive, fought hard for its survival.

Rabo had a feeling that was what he was going to have to do, too. That's what everybody on this little craft was going to have to do.

"What do these people have in mind?" João pressed his face against a portal and stared out at the sharp-crested waves. *With the Uppers.* He'd always wanted to be an Upper. Dreamt of becoming one, never imagining it was really possible. Only a pipedream.

Somehow he'd ended up here, with them. Yet not one of them. And they were off on some horrible journey from what Gason and Rabo had thus far intimated. "Where are we going?"

Rabo leapt off his bunk and appeared at the boy's side. "Cloudja said they are steering towards Cape Horn."

"Cape Horn!" João scoffed. "In this piece of garbage?" His head shook side to side in disbelief. What they'd planned was a deadly adventure. "We'll never make it. We'll be ripped to shreds, boat and all. They should have left me in the ocean and saved me the trouble of having to die again."

Would they die? Rabo wondered. Cloudja didn't seem to think so. But she said a lot had to do with this Hiel character and Rabo still wasn't sure who he was. Sounded like some kind of god.

And Rabo didn't believe in gods. There was a very good chance that Cloudja and her companion, Gason, were a couple of loons. Drifting about in the ocean, living in a fantasy land. Make that ocean.

That would explain a lot of things. Rabo drummed his fingers against the portal. Then again, how had he gotten here? In this world of Uppers and Lowers?

Maybe *he* was the loon.

Leaving João to his own bitter thoughts, Rabo quietly slipped away. Quill was sequestered in a separate cabin. It had been Cloudja's private room. She now shared it with the girl.

Rabo knocked delicately. There was no response. He hadn't expected any. Quill behaved as if she was barely alive. Knowing that Cloudja was above with Gason, Rabo opened the door and stepped into the dimly lit quarters. "Quill?"

He heard a rustling of the bedclothes. "It's me, Rabo."

After a moment's silence, the girl replied blandly. "Go away."

"I only wanted to see if you're okay—if you need anything."

"I don't need anything."

Rabo slowly let out his breath, his hand clutching the doorhandle. "I'll be going then." He turned to leave.

"There's things in my head." Quill's voice sounded tearful.

Rabo could make out the dark shadows of her hands pressing the sides of her head. He bit his lip. "What kind of things?" He could think of nothing more clever or helpful to say in response.

"Things. All kinds of things. Dark things, deep things. Scratching. Scratching, scratching. Scratching away at my brain." Quill sobbed. "At my eyes." She kicked the sheets off her legs. "They're killing me!"

Rabo rushed to her side and pulled her near-weightless form to his breast. "Don't worry," he said softly. "I'm here.

Everything will be all right."

Quill's chest shook and Rabo closed his eyes, invoking a silent prayer. There was so much going on. And he understood none of it.

And from what he saw and heard, none of it looked good—for any of them.

—28—

The rain stopped.

The air turned dry quickly, as if a voracious beast was sucking the moisture out of the atmosphere and out of his pores. George felt his skin growing brittle, his tongue parched. It didn't seem possible that anything could be so arid.

He wanted to ask questions, but his throat was too dry, too sore. The sand pulled at his feet. George didn't think life could get any worse than this. The heat seemed almost alive, like it was trying to knock him off his feet.

And then the winds picked up. Puffs of breeze quickly turned into savage hot winds sending sharp bits of sand biting into their exposed faces; hungry, angry little silica-based insects out to devour them.

The sandstorm swirled around, engulfing them. The figures of the others in the party quickly disappeared but for the nearest. Floadan sang and Cleea whistled. Their muffled voices kept the little band together.

George fought for each step. A low, dark shape appeared at his side. George peered at it through the gauzy mask he'd knotted over his eyes using a bit of clothing from his pack.

At first, it looked like nothing more than a tree stump, gnarled and weather beaten and George wondered how it could ever have grown there. But as George brushed past, it moved. A long arm, thick as a baseball bat, flinched and a rough brown hand surged out of cover of the sand and savagely grabbed his ankle.

George cried out, but his plaintive call was smothered as he was dragged deeper down into the sand. He fought with his arms; desperately kicked with his feet. The sand was thick and whatever had him by the ankle was too strong. George fell lower and lower until he felt certain he would smother.

Yet as suddenly as his ordeal had begun, it was over. George felt the painful grip on his left ankle pop loose. He tumbled into a deep, black hole. He heard a discomforting whistling—not the now familiar singsong-like whistling of the angels—but rather like a low boiling tea kettle and heard what sounded like feet shuffling.

But he could not see who or what it was. It was too dark to make out more than the hint of shapes down here.

George quietly probed the space behind him and found only empty air. So at least there was room to move. Maybe even to run if need be.

"Hello."

George's heart jumped up his throat. Whatever being had spoken had a thick, alien lisp. George stepped away from the direction from which he estimated the incorporeal voice had come.

"You meat." There was a scratching sound. "And no meat." A rude sniffling sound followed. "Different. You different."

Shuffling feet came towards George and he stepped away until his back was pressed against cool, rough rock. How the devil was the creature tracking him?

"Speaks you?"

George swallowed. His parched throat crackled as he sputtered. "W-who are you?" A cold wind rolled through the black tunnel as if the cave was alive and breathing.

"Ahhh." The voice sounded cheered. "Speaks you."

George quietly edged his way along the concavity. Maybe he could sneak away. But how was he going to get out of here and catch up with the others?

A thick lump suddenly pressed George against the rock, bruising his spine. "Speaks you," said the dark, lumpy shape in George's face.

George pushed the beast away and dug into his pack. He pulled out a light globe and held it out in front of him. He was in a massive, oval-shaped chamber, more than two hundred feet in circumference, by his guess.

The creature who had waylaid him stood an arm's length away. It was a sallow-colored thing, lumpy as a half-empty sack of flour with yellow, scaly skin. The odor it gave off—or was it the cave?—was reminiscent of suet. George's grandmother used to make candles from animal fat in her kitchen back on the family farm outside Lansing, Michigan. George thought it was disgusting then. It was even more disgusting now.

The creature cocked its thick head. Heavy folds of skin fell over its shoulders like voluminous draperies. It had two longish arms and two stumpy legs that looked more in keeping with an elephant's than a human's.

But the oddest of all was this creature's face which was dominated by a large, squat nose with huge nostrils from which a dense tangle of white hairs extended. It had an equally large mouth, rimmed with fat lips and apparently no teeth. None that George could see anyway.

What was it planning on doing? Swallowing George whole? With no teeth, the creature wasn't about to tear George to shreds. No. All he had to do, he decided, was stay out of its way. And with the light globe to guide him through the cave, that shouldn't be hard.

Especially since this subterranean devil had no eyes.

George moved to the right. His feet making no sound on the solid slab of which the floor was comprised. The creature mimicked him. George stopped, eyed the creature which had also stopped. George took a second step. The creature did the same.

And the same for a third and a fourth. George hesitated a moment. He broke off a pencil-thin stalk of stalagmite and sent it flying against the opposite wall. The creature turned its head in the direction of the crash.

George took this opportunity to run the opposite way. But the creature was not so stupid as George might have hoped. And it moved fast.

Faster than George.

Its corpulent figure blocked the narrow passage ahead, its thick lips rippling like a hungry octopus' tentacles.

George measured the distance between himself and a cluster of rocks in the other direction. There appeared to be a passageway up there. If he could reach it before this stinking beast. . .

"No run," said the creature. "No be afraid, meat. Yoli no eat meat. Eat this."

The creature, Yoli, dipped a hand in a shallow pool at its feet that George hadn't noticed until now. The thing's webbed hand came up with a pile of white slime or fungus of some sort. Heaven only knew. The creature brought an ooze-covered hand to his mouth and sucked the goo down his throat with oddly-disturbing, slurping noises.

"Meat talk. Yoli talk meat."

"Y-you mean you want to talk?"

Yoli nodded.

George's muscles relaxed a bit. "Are you responsible for my being here?" This Yoli certainly looked nothing like whatever it was that had nabbed him. The thing that had snatched him from the surface had a hide as brown and hard as tree bark. Yoli looked practically gelatinous.

"Xoxo bring you."

"Xoxo?"

Yoli sank into the pool, let his hands play with the water. "Xoxo is my extension."

"Your extension?"

Yoli tipped his head toward the roof of the cave. "He doesn't like it." Yoli lowered his voice and said, "He doesn't even know about my Xoxo. If He finds out, he will kill my Xoxo."

"He who?" George had no idea what this now pathetic looking creature was rambling on about, but figured the sooner he humored it, the sooner he'd be on his way.

"Lord of the Deep Refuge," whispered Yoli. "Not say His name."

George felt the skin along his stomach burn, felt the black whip cutting him in two. Hiel. This creature was talking about Hiel.

"You know this Lord of the Deep Refuge, do you?" replied George, struggling to keep his voice steady.

"I talk to Him once. Long time ago. He not like what Yoli speaks. But he cannot kill Yoli so he sends Yoli here. To these caves." His voice turned sad. "These endless, endless caves. . ."

"Where is here," asked George, "exactly?"

Yoli's fat lips rolled from side to side. "Cannot say for certain. This is the Underside. He keeps me here." Yoli inched closer, his voice dropped. "But I have my Xoxo. Xoxo gives me sight."

"What do you see?"

A sound that could only have been a giggle crossed the odd creature's lips. "I tell you what I told Him." Yoli's neck angled toward the cavern roof.

"Okay."

"I tell him I see a George and I see a Claire."

George gasped. Claire! Was this possible? He grabbed hold of the creature's shoulders. "What about this Claire? What about George?"

"I tell Him that He is dead soon. I tell him that George going to kill Him." Yoli's voice was low and carried a sense of foreboding. Yoli's hands grabbed hold of George's. "You George."

George nodded.

Yoli bobbed up and down. "I feel it. Come." He turned and began walking.

"Tell me, Yoli," said George, matching the creature step for step, "what about Claire?"

Yoli paused and turned. "Claire sees, too. Claire your Xoxo, George?" Yoli resumed walking.

"I-I don't know. . ."

The sands settled, but it was no welcome sight.

"We're surrounded," scowled Artegan, one of the captains of their forces.

Cleea nodded. "So I see." Indeed, their small army was completed encircled by an army ten times in size. It was as if they'd been swallowed whole and waited now only to be digested.

"What happened to Ungris?" grumbled Lancemaster Servil. "Why did we receive no warning?"

"Ungris has let us down," grumbled Artegan.

"Let us down," said Cleea, evenly, "or has Ungris and his party been captured and destroyed?" She let out a soft breath. "Sharan was among them."

Artegan lowered his head. "My apologies, Cleea. You are right."

Cleea scanned the faces. "And where is George?"

Floadan spoke up. "He's disappeared. I lost sight of him in the sandstorm. I hoped he was here with you."

Cleea shook her head. "I've not seen him."

With this news, chaos broke out.

"Quiet!" commanded Cleea. "We must not lose sight of who and what we are. Thudor cannot frighten us. Not even the Lord of the Deep Refuge can sway us from our purpose."

"But without George—" began Captain Artegan.

"We will do what is required of us," said Cleea sternly.

"But there are so many of them," groaned a nearby soldier under the captain's command. "What can we do?"

Cleea looked at the liquid horizon. Thudor's vast army was marching—straight for them. "We fight," she said. "We fight like there's no tomorrow." And very possibly there would be no tomorrow.

Floadan pulled his sword from his scabbard and held it high. "I am ready."

"Wait." Cleea laid a hand on Floadan's shoulder. "We must prepare. We must map our attack."

Floadan grinned. "Just follow me."

"No, Floadan. You must not—"

Floadan cried out, "For the Eye Of The World and our Queen!"

He charged towards the enemy.

—29—

Their small boat was pulled, batted and swatted along the deadly and desolate tip of South America.

Rabo, not a fan of boats to begin with, was constantly seasick. He gazed at the barren landscape and longed to set foot there.

He had not spotted a solitary ship besides their own the entire voyage. Gason said that few vessels, if any, dared venture beyond the main cities. "Too many dangers," he'd explained. "The Lowers, you know."

Rabo nodded, though he didn't understand quite what those dangers were.

And Rabo had seen little of his companions, though Cloudja and Gason frequently visited him in his cabin. From them, he learned that João was as stubborn and difficult as ever, while Quill remained in her own cabin, mumbling and muttering as she dreamed and tossed fitfully in her bunk.

Rabo also learned that their small vessel was headed for what Cloudja called an induction zone—a vent of some sort—off the western coast of the continent. He didn't understand what she meant, but then he didn't object or complain either. He was only along for the ride.

Rabo also kept this information to himself. Quill wouldn't have cared. She was much too catatonic to care about anything.

But the news would have stoked João's smoldering ire. For Cloudja and Gason had some mad plan—a plan he couldn't fathom—to enter this so-called induction vent, sending them all straight to the bottom of the sea and into the center of the earth!

This would certainly get them all killed.

Rabo didn't care.

At this point, all he knew for certain—his world, his home—was gone. If dying was next on the agenda, then so be it, he concluded. He would die on this one great, preposterous adventure. And so what if he died? By all rights he should be dead now anyway.

Rabo coughed up some salty, brown-green bile and turned away from the smudged and damp portal. Gason had given him some tea with peppermint oil that was supposed to calm his stomach. He poured a generous cupful from a heavy kettle and swallowed it down in one hot gulp.

It burned all the way down his throat and the strong oil made his nostrils flare and his eyes water.

Cloudja came in. "You are still troubled." The Queen

wore the same gown as always. Neither she nor Gason had once changed their garments in all the days they seemed to have traveled. How many days, Rabo could not judge. He'd been in and out of consciousness, barely aware of his own body, let alone his surroundings.

Rabo nodded and sat up. "I'll survive." His insides made loud gurgling noises. But how long? he wondered.

"Gason says we will be at our destination shortly."

"What happens then?" She made to reply but he cut her off. "Never mind. I don't want to know."

Cloudja came closer and laid her hand over his. "The truth is, I don't know for certain myself what will happen. So much is unknowable. So much is at stake. The Eye of the World depends on us. On us all."

Cloudja's fingers rapped lightly atop Rabo's knuckles. "The Lord of the Deep Refuge will try to stop us. There will likely be a battle."

Rabo puffed out his emaciated chest. "I'll do my part."

The Queen smiled. "You already have."

"How's that?"

"You brought us all together as was intended."

Rabo's brow knitted into a tight knot. "I don't understand. Why am I here? Why are any of us here? What can I do besides lie around being seasick?"

She smiled. "Everything is interconnected in this life. Everything we do, everything we feel," her hand ran along the edge of his bunk, "everything we touch. All is connected. If you hadn't had your accident, none of this could have happened."

He looked confused.

"We would not be here now." She glanced out the portal at the tossing sea. "Where we need to be."

A sudden thought struck Rabo and he asked, "Are you responsible for my being here? Did you cause that accident?"

"No. That is beyond me. Perhaps we did it together."

Rabo frowned. Nothing she said made any sense.

"Who knows what else we might accomplish."

"But—"

The boat was suddenly tossed to port and Cloudja was thrown forward. Rabo caught her in his arms. "Are you okay?"

Cloudja nodded. "Thank you." She patted his hand. "Rest." With that one word, she took her leave.

Rabo threw himself down on his queasy stomach with a sigh. She hadn't really answered any of his questions to his satisfaction.

By accident or design?

His stomach groaned. Possibly she had no real answers to give him. His soul might be starving, but there was solid food for his body.

George and Yoli plodded through the cold, dark corridor. They had entered a particularly damp stretch with transparent liquid glistening off the rock. The air smelled of ionized summer rain.

Yoli was explaining how Hiel, Lord of the Deep Refuge,

had summoned him to His fortress. He'd heard how Yoli knew things and had a sight that went beyond what mere eyes could see.

"I told the Lord that I saw His hand subvert the Eye of the World. That pleased Him." Yoli's feet made no sound as they crossed over the bare rock, while George's own less sure steps echoed up and back through the seemingly endless tract of tunnel etched through the dense rock.

"He kept me by His side a long time. I did not like it. I did not like being there. But He gives one no choice."

"So how did you end up here?"

Yoli replied. "I told Him that while I saw Him succeeding at much, that ultimately He would fail."

George chuckled. "I'll bet Hiel took that real well."

"You shouldn't say His name," cautioned Yoli. "He does not like this."

"Tough."

"As you wish, George," said Yoli. "But I caution you: If you say His name, He will hear you. And He will find you."

Memories of cold sweats and nightmarish dreams came to mind. George relived the burning pain of Hiel's black whip searing his flesh, cleaving his body in two.

George told Yoli he'd be more careful. It wasn't that he cared so much about himself, but if Hiel found George, poor Yoli could be in trouble, too.

"To answer your question: The Lord would have killed me then, struck me down if He could."

"And He couldn't?"

"No. This is not possible."

"Why not?" If Hiel was as powerful as everybody kept alluding to, why couldn't he squash a blind little fellow like this defenseless Yoli?

Yoli paused a moment at a bifurcation in the rock. George held his light orb out and saw only darkness in either direction. "Yoli not alive. Can't kill what does not live."

"I don't understand," began George, "how can you not be alive when—"

Yoli held up his hand. "We must not speak now. There are others."

George tensed. "Others?" he whispered.

Yoli nodded. "They come."

George squinted but made out nothing but blackness. Not a sound could be heard.

"You should put away your light, George," said Yoli. "Until we know the nature of our guests."

George couldn't agree more. He stuffed the orb into his pack.

"Take my hand, George." George did so and Yoli pulled him along. They snaked in near silence along a corridor so narrow that George's arms and shoulders were scraped raw.

The battle above ground was quick and merciless.

Thudor smiled. He stood in the entrance of his field headquarters, a giant triangular tent set up on a rise looking down upon Orexis. He was a gaunt figure, cut from a flawed cloth, or so his master was fond of saying. Thudor took this as a compliment. His thoughts ran from the battle to more pressing matters.

Somewhere out there was George. He'd had him once and he'd slipped away. He could not afford to let that happen again. Hiel had been furious. Another failure would cost Thudor his existence. Hiel had made that plain.

Thudor's black eyes gazed across the Steppes of Orexis, his eyes searching out his quarry. "The fools," he muttered, "like sheep to the slaughter they come."

"Still," said Bumbold, a gray, slithery-skinned creature with teeth made for tearing flesh and claw-like hands meant for rending its still breathing prey into bite-sized pieces, "they fight well."

A sneer passed across Thudor's half-hidden face. "Then they shall die well." He smiled, his right hand rubbing the onyx-handled staff he carried in his left. "The Lord of the Deep Refuge will be pleased."

Thudor tapped his staff against the ground sending up a shower of sulfurous sparks. The dry brown grass about his feet burned a moment then gave up. "Very pleased."

Thudor swivelled on Bumbold. "See that no one remains alive. Tell the troops I want nothing left. Nothing and no one."

Bumbold nodded and raced from the tent towards the center of the fighting. By the time he arrived, there was little reason for him to relay Thudor's orders, for very few of the enemy now remained standing.

"Floadan!" shouted Cleea. "It's too late. We must flee!"

The bloodstained warrior's sword flinched as he slashed at yet another of Thudor's thugs. The faceless thing fell over at his feet. "No, we cannot give up. Cloudja depends on us. The Eye of the World depends on us!"

"Don't you think I know that?" Cleea and Floadan fought side to side. A small group of them, all that remained of their army, had been forced up into the jagged rocks, driven there by Thudor's ceaseless hoard. "But we need reinforcements."

"We need George," grumbled Floadan, fighting for breath as they struggled up the rocks.

An archer named Taitian, with a short bow in one hand, let loose an arrow. It found its mark. "Perhaps he has returned to his home."

Cleea's face darkened. "No, he would not do that. He came when we called him. He would not leave us now in this time of our dire need."

Two more of their troops fell. A towering Llorri ran towards them. Before anyone could respond, the giant had wrapped his arm around Cleea's neck.

She dropped her sword and was forced to fight back with her hands. Taitian dropped her bow and pulled her knife free. With Cleea and the Llorri wrestling about she was going to have to wait for the right moment to find her target.

But Floadan wasn't waiting. With a chilling cry, he hurled himself at the gray giant. For a moment, the three of them hung there and then the Llorri fell to the ground. Floadan hit him over and over about the neck and face with a large, flat stone.

Cleea scrambled to her feet. She looked about wildly and found her sword wedged between two rocks. While she struggled to loosen it, Taitian threw herself on the fallen Llorri who was now fighting his way to his feet. Floadan had dropped his stone and clung to the giant's leg, trying in desperation to bring him down.

The Llorri laughed, plucked Floadan by his shirt and sent him sailing against a jagged outcropping of rock.

"No!" shouted Cleea. But it was too late. Floadan's back struck the rock. For a moment he gazed at them in surprise. Then he fell lifelessly to earth, his back broken.

Cleea threw her blade at the Llorri's chest. It penetrated to the hilt and the giant faltered then fell to his knees. A hand grabbed her arm before she could rush at the giant to finish him off or at least try. She knew how difficult it was to actually kill one of the fabled Llorri.

She turned to her attacker, hands at the ready, then gasped in surprise. "Ungris!"

He nodded. "Hurry!" Ungris waved to the others. "In here!"

Cleea, Taitian and the handful of those left, hastened through a narrow crack in the rocks. A cold breeze hit their faces.

"Come on," urged Ungris. "We've got to get back. Away from the entrance."

Potaster stood just inside the entrance, his hands gripped tightly against a massive boulder.

"Everybody in?" asked Ungris.

Cleea nodded.

"Now," said Ungris, motioning to his giant friend.

Potaster tightened his jaw and pulled at the rock. At first nothing seemed to happen. But after what seemed like time enough for entire civilizations to have risen and fallen, the boulder budged and, with a scraping sound that echoed through the chamber, the rock fell, starting a small avalanche that effectively blocked the entrance.

A shadowy figured pulled a light orb from her pack lifting the veil of blackness that had engulfed them.

"Sharan!" Cleea rushed to her friend's side and hugged her. "You are well. You're all well. Tell, me, what happened?" The sounds of frustrated savagery filtered through from the outside as their attackers tried to get at them.

Sharan explained how their scouting expedition had been spotted and they had come close to being captured and killed. "We found this spot and were trying to find a way back to you when the battle broke out."

"I'm sorry we couldn't be of more service," lamented Ungris. He looked about the small, bedraggled assembly. "Where is my cousin, Floadan?"

Cleea approached Ungris and took his hand. "Floadan saved my life. You can be very proud."

Ungris's head dipped and his lips moved in prayer. Suddenly his sharp eyes hardened. "And what about George? Where is George?"

Cleea looked helpless. She shook her head. "I don't know,

Ungris. He's disappeared."

Ungris cursed. "Good riddance. Worthless to begin with. Don't know why I bothered to pluck him from Thudor's grip.

"Please, Ungris—"

Potaster, who had been in constant motion adding rock to the opening, interrupted, saying, "I suggest we move away from here. They seem most determined to come after us." He looked about. "And I seem to be running out of useful material to block their desire."

Cleea took in their cold, empty surroundings. Not much of a defense could be mounted here. "I see what you mean." She turned to Sharan. "Is there another way out of here?"

"Not that we've yet found."

Ungris added, "But these blasted caves go on for miles." As the sound of digging outside rose, he cursed them all to hell. He spat. "I should know, I've trudged along half of them."

"Then we'd better get started." The sounds of Thudor's army digging towards them grew louder as they had apparently picked up their pace. "And be hopeful," said Cleea. "All is not yet lost."

Ungris begged to differ but kept his yap shut.

−30−

Tim drove slowly, keeping his eyes on the road, the sidewalks, each passing car.

Where was Dad?

Tim stopped for gas on Federal Highway and drove north.

For no particular reason.

He had to go somewhere. Had to look someplace. Dad could be anywhere.

Dad could be dead.

"No," he muttered, his hands strangling the wheel of the Volvo, "not dead." He chased the thought away. Dad couldn't be dead. Tim wouldn't let him die.

He drove up Federal Highway all the way out to Jupiter then cruised home along A1A which followed the Atlantic. Tim shook his head. Claire and her goofy ideas. Did she really think Dad was under the ocean somewhere? With angels?

He looked at his watch and realized it was getting late. Soon it would be dark. Mom might start looking for him. She'd probably already be having a fit that he was gone in the first place.

Tim turned inland and started home. Who knows, he thought, maybe Dad will be waiting at the dinner table when I get there.

But he didn't believe it for a minute, not even for a second.

The ridiculously small vessel rode up a massive wave, then plunged down the other side. Rabo clung to the sides of his bunk.

Gason appeared in the doorway. "There's a storm coming up."

Rabo looked at Gason in disbelief. "You've got a knack for understatement, you know that?"

Gason smiled. "Glad to see you've got some fight in you. The sea hasn't taken that away."

"No, only my lunch." Rabo propped himself up on his elbows. "And my breakfast and my dinner and everything else I've tried to keep down today."

Gason nodded and handed Rabo some rain gear. "Cloudja needs you."

Rabo wanted to refuse but found he couldn't. No point in being useless. If he could be of value to someone or something, no matter how little he understood of it, he would do so. "I'm coming."

Marching along behind Gason in the narrow passage, Rabo heard Quill's wails. "Is she alright?"

Gason answered without slowing. "She is weak but will survive. It is her misfortune to be in the wrong place at the wrong time."

Rabo nodded. "Aren't we all."

They stepped up onto the deck. Rabo sucked in a breath. The sky was black as coal. Not a star could be seen. Was it day or night?

A freezing rain fell in sheets that created a roar as the drops pounded the teak deck.

And there in the center of it all stood Cloudja. Soaked to the bones, wet hair flying in every direction, eyes focused on the blackness above.

"What is she doing?" whispered Rabo, clutching the rail as the boat plunged down yet another massive wave and lurched to starboard.

"She is trying to see."

"Good luck," grumbled Rabo. "What is it you want me to do, hold her umbrella?"

Gason tugged Rabo's shoulder and indicated a slumped figure near the helm. "It's the boy."

Rabo fought to clear the cold rain from his eyes. "João?" The boy sat in the corner, covered in a rain slicker, knees pulled up to his chest. Wet and miserable looking. "Is he okay?"

"Cloudja needs him. We approach our destination. He has discovered us and our objective."

"You mean this Lord of the Deep Refuge guy?"

Gason nodded. "There is only one who can aid us and Cloudja says we cannot connect with him without the boy's help. Without it, I fear we are doomed. The Eye of the World is doomed."

Rabo feared they were all doomed no matter what. "What do you want me to do?" He was shouting. It was the only way to make himself heard over the roar of the storm.

"He's your friend. He's of this world of yours. Can you not talk to him?"

Rabo studied Cloudja. Her arms were extended out and upward. How she kept her feet in place with the bucking of the boat and churning of the waves, he couldn't begin to fathom. But he knew he had to help her.

Rabo turned his attention back to Gason. "What is it you want me to say to him exactly?"

Gason shrugged. "I do not know, Rabo."

Rabo scrambled over to where João was huddled and pressed up against him. "Hey, João. How you doing? Some storm, huh?"

After a moment, João spoke. "I want to go home."

"We all want to go home, buddy." He laid a hand over the boy's shoulders. They sat wordlessly for many minutes listening to the thundering rain and hurricane winds that engulfed them, threatened to destroy them.

"I know," said Rabo, "maybe if we think about home that might help." He forced a smile. "Maybe we can think ourselves home. What do you say?"

"I say life stinks," Joan replied sullenly.

A sharp cry shattered the air. It was Quill. Rabo bit his lip. Poor Quill. The storm was driving her even madder. He looked to Gason for support but Gason had his back to him as he struggled to steer the boat. A hopeless task if ever there was one.

A trace of lightning, as big as the sky, appeared one moment and was gone the next.

Cloudja drew her arms in close to her sides and closed her eyes. Rabo could see her lips moving but had no idea what she was saying. He hoped she was praying because that seemed about the only thing left to do.

—31—

Tim found his mother asleep on the sofa.

The TV droned in the background. Nothing but gray fuzz. His mother's face was all puffy, like she'd been crying. Tim sighed. "Poor Mom." He'd come back and send her to bed after he checked on Claire.

He tiptoed to Claire's room. Her door was open a crack and he pushed it wider. His little sister sat slumped over her desk, a yellow crayon in her hand.

Tim pushed her head gently to one side and looked at the drawing. He shook his head. "Bizarre," he muttered.

He gave Claire a gentle nudge. It took several tries before she awoke. When she did, her eyes popped open wide and she gasped. "Timmy! I'm so glad you're home! I figured it out!"

She grabbed his hand and wouldn't let go.

"Figured what out?"

She snatched her latest drawing from the desktop and stuck it in front of his nose.

He took it by the corners and turned it side to side, studying it carefully. "What's it supposed to be?"

A gray, leathery-skinned creature bounded out from the darkness and sank its teeth into George's neck. He fought it off. The fierce little thing scrambled to its feet and came again. "What is this?" George hollered, barely able to make out his attacker in the near pitch blackness.

"One of Thudor's pets," said Yoli, his voice suddenly more shrill than usual. "I feel you, Bumbold. Would you like me to feel you?"

The horrid creature fell from George and dusted itself off. He looked at Yoli with both fear and insolence combined. "Yoli. So this is where Hiel sent you." The creature turned to George. "And you give aid to His greatest enemy. He will not be pleased."

Yoli smiled. "It has never been my destiny to please the Lord of the Deep Refuge, it seems." He crouched. "Now, go! Before I embrace you."

Bumbold sized up his opponent, turned on his heels and was gone. His challenge echoed up the tunnel. "The end is near, George. Hiel seeks your audience. And when He is finished so shall you be."

Yoli pressed into a nondescript opening in the tunnel. "This is where you must go."

George looked inside. An enormous cavern greeted him.

Empty but for two shafts of light, one red, one blue. The mesmerizing lights circled each other like they were performing some perpetual dance. Perhaps they'd been dancing that way for hundreds of years, perhaps tens of thousands.

Yoli stepped aside. "This is your path, George."

George's eyes followed the strangely compelling shafts of light. They reminded him of those magnificent and puzzling red and blue stones he had seen embedded in the floor of the Eye Of The World back in the city of Ryaii.

What did it all mean?

The sound of running steps and clattering weapons grew louder. The racket was coming from the direction George and Yoli had come.

"The Lord of the Deep Refuge has found you, George." Yoli was shimmered now, a bundle of semi-translucent and glittering purple. "You must leave."

George watched in wonder as a long spear, as long as himself, hit Yoli, glowed then slowly disappeared. "Are-are you all right?"

Yoli nodded. "Though it is best not to talk now, George. They come now. From both directions."

George drew his short sword. He peered vainly into the surrounding darkness. In frustration, he drew his light orb from his pack, brought it to life and hurled it down the tunnel. There were shouts and Thudor's troops rushed at them like a tidal wave.

George held his sword out before him and shouted. As he

did, several bodies flew past him. At first he thought they were more of Hiel's army, but they threw themselves into the fray and engaged the enemy.

He recognized their faces. "Cleea!"

She turned briefly and smiled, then returned to her attacker.

George raced to their aid. "Sharan, Ungris! You're all right!"

"Shut up and help us, you sentimental idiot!" oathed Ungris as he upended a Llorri who wasn't in a hurry to give up the battle.

Potaster threw himself on his kin and put an end to the argument.

The sounds of fighting filled the tunnel but something louder rumbled in the distance.

"What are you all doing here?" demanded George. "How did you get here?"

Cleea pulled George back from the fighting. "Thudor has defeated us, George. It is up to you now." Her hand gripped his wrist. "What will you do?"

Yoli was pushing forward. Thudor's men seemed to fear him and tried vainly to keep out of his way. Those that were not fortunate enough to succeed turned to liquid pools of gelatinous rot from which not even their screams had time to escape. "Listen to Cleea, George. You must follow your path."

George looked into the open chamber. Red circled blue, around and around and around. The sound of a deep rumbling penetrated his thoughts. "What is that?"

"Hiel has found you, George."

Yoli had spoken His name. Too late for precautions, figured George.

Cleea's eyes pleaded with George. "What you hear is the water, George. It comes. Hiel has sent it. Soon it—"

A wall of water came crashing around the bend and both armies cried in surprise. Frightened screams filled George's ears. Was he responsible for all this death?

Cleea pulled George close and kissed him. "Please help us, George."

He nodded and took a step towards the chamber, drawn to the circling red and blue lights, like a moth to the flame. The flame of death.

What was going to happen when he got closer to the lights? Should he touch them? He heard voices, tiny spirit voices that lit on his brain like hummingbird's wings, like those he'd encountered at the blue fountain in Ryaii.

Should he wait here and see what happens? He turned to Cleea, his angel. "What am I supposed to do?"

She was gone.

The raging water burst into the chamber, carrying the bodies of both friends and foes—living or dead, he could not tell— and tossed George into the lights.

There was a brilliant flash of light.

And George was falling.

−32−

"It's the water," explained Claire. "Can't you see?"

She grabbed the paper away from Tim. "And this is the Devil and this is his—"

"You're crazy," Tim muttered. "Just like Dad." He went to the door and stopped. Claire was crying. He sighed and went to her. "I'm sorry. I didn't mean that."

"Yes, you did. You think Daddy's crazy, just like Mommy does."

"Listen, nobody thinks Dad is crazy, okay?"

Claire sniffled.

"We're all worried about him, that's all." He gazed at Claire's weird drawing on the desk. "Tell me about this again."

"Well," Claire swallowed her tears, "this is the Devil and he has this power." A long black and yellow line ran from the black devil's hand to a tall shape near the center of the page.

Tim tapped the paper. "What's this?"

"That's the Eye."

"The Eye?"

She nodded.

Tim scratched his head. "Looks more like a lighthouse to me."

"Well, it's the Eye. And the Devil wants it and Daddy has to keep him from getting it."

Tim slumped down on Claire's bed. His head throbbed. This didn't make any sense.

Nothing made any sense anymore.

He rubbed his face. "And Dad's with this Devil and they're fighting?"

She nodded again.

"And you see all this?"

Her head barely moved. Claire's words came out a whisper. "You don't believe me."

Claire's clock ticked off the seconds.

Tim came to his feet and bent over his little sister's drawing. His finger traced the edges of the edifice in the center, being struck by some sort of huge lightning bolt. "This looks like a lighthouse."

"Lighthouse?"

"Yeah. Like the one up in Jupiter. I passed it on my drive. When I was looking for Dad. Could this be that lighthouse?"

Claire shrugged.

Tim grabbed her hand and pulled her to the garage.

"Where are we going?"

"We're going to get Dad." Tim snatched the key to the Volvo from the hook and told Claire to hop in.

The garage door opened as he started up the engine. "Where do you two think you're going?" shouted Mrs. Richards.

"We're going to find Dad!" shouted Claire and Tim as one.

"What? You get back here. Are you out of your minds?"

Tim backed the car out onto the drive. Drops of rain spattered across the windshield. The storm that had been threatening all day had finally come for them.

"Tim!" Their mother stepped off the stoop and raised her hand. "You come back here! You don't know what you're doing!"

Quill screamed again. She knocked over Rabo who'd been trying to calm her, and raced unprotected up onto the deck, into the center of the storm.

She threw herself at Cloudja. Cloudja remained steady on her feet, her hands aimed at the Heavens.

"I'll get her!" Rabo shouted as he shot past Gason. But Cloudja's companion stopped him.

"No," he said, his eyes filled with a sudden comprehension. "Let her go. Leave Quill be."

"What? She's messing everything up!"

Gason shook his head slowly, a smile dared to appear across his visage. "She is the one."

"But—"

"Look."

Rabo did.

The storm doubled its fury. Rain tore at his flesh, wind etched his bones. And Quill and Cloudja held hands.

The sky filled with brilliant flashes of light. One passed overhead. Then another.

A deadly yellow bolt, jagged as death, grew in the distance. Rabo had no doubt it was headed for them.

And he had no doubt that it carried death.

For them all.

The air sizzled and the bolt came as if in slow motion. Cloudja was saying some bizarre ritual that Rabo couldn't hope to understand. João cowered uselessly in the corner. Gason held the boat's helm. A useless task in this mother of all storms.

The bolt came straight for Rabo's heart. Of all the things he hadn't understood these past few confusing days, of that he was certain.

Quill shouted with every fiber of her body. Her hand shot up.

—33—

George was vertiginous.

He was falling. He was certain of it. Yet all he saw were streaks of white light. What did it mean?

Was this it?

Was this what it was like to finally go completely nuts? Dr. Grossman, are you there?

Was he dying?

The answer hit him feet first. He struck something solid and came to a stop, breathless and dizzy. Queasy.

The light that had surrounded him disappeared.

A shadowy, boulder strewn landscape spread out in every direction. Cleea! Sharan! He swivelled his head. Where was everybody?

He stopped. "Where am I?" He was standing naked but for tattered cotton pajama bottoms on an inhospitable planetoid covered with a gray, rocky desert.

In the distance, a black monolith beckoned and brought a fear and dread to him all in the same instant. He wanted to run as much as he knew he needed to go forward.

This was just like his dream.

And he did go forward, barefoot over the hot, rocky desert. As he approached the monolith, it became clear that this was a fortress, an ugly and imposing one, stretching from one edge of the horizon to the other.

George was sweating. George was scared to death. Yet on he marched, his feet growing bloody, his body growing weaker.

And then the realization of his predicament fell on him like a bucket of horrors.

George's breath caught in his throat. This cold, dark place was Hiel's place. "Lord of the Deep Refuge."

As if in response to his naming, from the far left, a gray smudge quickly appeared in the impossibly high ramparts, then closed just as suddenly. A huge creature, like a giant robot monster from one of the sci-fi comic books he'd read as a child, rode out on a black chariot. Its wheels were nearly two meters high and half a meter wide. Rocks turned to dust under its treads. The robot looking creature was black, too, and carried a long whip in one massive hand.

Just like his dream.

As the creature drew closer, it was apparent that chariot and driver were one. The beast was half chariot, half robot and half something else—something powerful and cunning.

As large as it was, it managed to bear down on George in

only seconds, kicking up rocks and dust in the thin, alien air.

And George knew what would happen next. It would be just like his dreams.

Hi-el. Remember me, George. Hiel. Fear me, George.

A layer of sweat formed on George's skin. Already Hiel's presence penetrated his mind, taunting him with his words.

Hi-el. Do not forget, George. Hiel. Fear me, George. Go back or face your doom.

He heard the angels, too. This time he recognized Cleea's angelic voice. *Save us, George. Please.*

George set his jaw and tensed up as Hiel spun in a circle around him, kicking up rocks as big as his skull.

George coughed, his lungs filling with sand. He spat and stood his ground. The big arm drew back over the monster's right shoulder. The black whip swung back like a headless snake, twisting and coiling in the throes of death. The arm snapped forward and the black whip, thick as George's forearm, lashed out at him like a hot, giant blue-black tongue.

The tip of the whip bit into George's flesh, scalding his skin and tearing open his belly.

George cried out in pain and clutched his belly. Hiel's arm drew back and the whip curled over his shoulder like a writhing snake. Again, Hiel sent it sailing in George's direction and he felt the sting of its bite.

George sank to his knees. He was being sliced in two and there wasn't a damn thing he could do about it.

The rain pelted them as they ran from the car. Tim started

running for the lighthouse but Claire stopped him.

"No, the beach. We have to go to the beach!" She pulled him forward.

The wind and rain whipped through them like glass shards as they hurried towards the beach. Was it possible? Was Dad out here somewhere?

Lightning struck a palm not ten feet from where Claire stood. She screamed.

"Watch out!" cried Tim. "This is getting dangerous. Way too dangerous. We'd better go back."

"No, we have to stay here." Claire ran to the smoldering tree, unfurled her drawing, snatched two crayons, one red and one blue from her pocket and began drawing.

"Are you—" Tim stopped himself. He was going to say crazy, then thought better of it.

He huddled beneath the smoldering tree hoping that lightning wouldn't strike the same place twice. At least not on the same night.

Using his hand to shield his eyes from the blinding storm, he searched desperately for some sign of their father.

George spit out a mouthful of sand. His face had been driven into the ground by Hiel's relentless and deadly whip. "Get it over with, already," he grumbled.

Hiel laughed. *George, George. You spoil the game. I expected more from you.*

"I expected more from myself," said George, struggling up from his knees.

Claire looked at her drawing. There was the Eye. And there was Daddy. And there was the Devil and the Devil was beating Daddy. "Stupid Devil." Her crayon drew her father's arms snatching the Devil's soul.

"Die, Devil!" Claire cried in frustration, driving her crayon through the Devil's heart. If he has one, she thought.

Rabo was horrified. Quill's hand reached for the bolt. She'd be killed, ten billion bolts, fried in an instant. Then again, they'd all be dead anyway.

The bolt shot overhead and Quill, still screaming her head off, snatched it and squeezed. She turned incandescent and Cloudja wasn't letting go of her grip on the girl's other bone-thin hand.

A wave the size of Sugarloaf was the last thing Rabo saw before being swept under with his shipmates.

The Eye of the World opened overhead. George saw the blue fountain. Heard voices. Elaine? Was that Elaine crying? What was wrong? Tim was calling his name.

George. Help us, George, called the angels.

And Claire was telling him something? What was it? He strained to hear.

Hiel's whip came for him again, sending him spinning and the Eye of the World disappeared in a swirl, as quickly as it had come.

Fear me, George. All is lost.

The hot pain seared his back. George struggled to remain conscious. He was being ripped apart until soon there would be nothing left.

Claire's voice appeared in his head. *Reach out, Daddy. Reach out.*

What?

Please, Daddy.

George rubbed his eyes. Hiel was rearing up on his chariot. He had come closer. Preparing to finish him off, no doubt.

As if reading George's mind, Hiel's whip circled overhead in a languid, deadly fashion, then lashed out.

George held his breath and waited.

The black whip came at him like a viper's tongue.

At the last possible moment, George grabbed at the whip. Hiel shouted angrily and pulled the whip away. It slipped in George's grip, but he managed to keep hold of it.

The whip tautened and turned bright yellow. An odd contrast in this otherwise gray and black world.

The length of the whip turned to flame. Hiel strove to turn his chariot aside but, with George holding on to the whip, was unable to do so. And Hiel either could not or would not let go of his end.

The flames grew larger. George felt the fire engulf him. In a moment, fire was all he could see. All he could feel.

And then there was water everywhere. The deluge of all deluges. The fire was out. Hiel's mad shouts were drowned out as chariot and driver sizzled and blew apart.

The entire planetoid seemed to have plunged into a universe of water instead of empty space, as impossible as that was.

George choked.

He was drowning. Suspended helplessly in the swirling waters. George had a glimpse of the Eye of World swimming free and unharmed, untarnished. Hiel gone.

Cleea swam toward him, saying, "It's okay to go home, George." She kissed him for the second time. "Thank you."

Other faces swam by, Sharan waved, Potaster waved, even grouchy Ungris said goodbye. And there were other faces George didn't recognize. Was that woman in white the famous Cloudja? She swirled around him in a loving embrace and disappeared in a shimmer of impossible light.

And he got colder and colder and colder. And the voices called and called and called. And it got darker and darker and darker. And George felt his lungs bursting and his capillaries bursting and his head bursting and then everything was getting light again like his whole mind was exploding.

And George dove and dove and dove.

And George knew that he was living. . .

—34—

George woke up, dazed and confused, with the texture of sand under his skin, the warm feel of sun on his face and the comforting scent of the ocean in his nostrils.

He pulled himself up out of the surf.

The sun was just coming up.

Where am I?

He studied the shoreline. It looked vaguely familiar. And then he recognized the lighthouse. The Jupiter lighthouse. Not bad. He wasn't too far from home at all. Fifty miles maybe.

George stood. His muscles were sore but he was all right. More than all right. His clothing was in tatters. But his soul seemed to have been patched up. Better than patched up. Remade.

George spotted a couple of children huddled up and sleeping under a charred palm tree. "Strange place and time for a couple of children to be out," he muttered. "Better make sure they're okay."

George started walking in their direction. His eyes turned to fountains of tears as he recognized the two sleeping figures. "Tim! Claire!"

George's walk turned to a sprint. He was home. And the world was right again.

Not a gray cloud in sight.

Also available from Beachfront

IT'S A YOUNG, YOUNG WORLD
by Glenn Meganck

*"It's A Young, Young World by Glenn Meganck is the story of an aging American senator and his compatriots who are mysteriously drawn by a scientist's dying words about the secret of eternal youth and the ability to live forever. Struggling to keep up in a youthful world, retiring Senator Chauncy and his 20-something bride purse an opportunity to recapture the power and excitement of youth in this fast-paced, wryly told, deftly written adventure laced with a very special insight into today's youth-centric culture. **Highly recommended**."* Midwest Book Review

It's a young world and Senator Robert Chauncy is old and getting older. Soon to be retired, the senator and his young bride are off to Florida for a little honeymoon. But his wife, Sheila, has a wandering eye and Fate has other surprises for them as well. On their way down the eastern seaboard, Sen. Chauncy finds himself trying to rescue a drowning man. The stranger dies, but before passing away, he baffles the senator and the gathered spectators with a mad tale of living forever. At first, his words are taken for those of a man in caught in delirium. But it is soon discovered that the seemingly middle-aged dead man was in reality an eccentric and elderly foreign scientist named Titus Olshenski. Sen. Chauncy and the others begin to wonder if Olshenski's dying words carry some hidden meaning. Did Olshenski have the key to the Fountain of Youth? Can the scientist's riddle be unlocked? Can they find the Fountain of Youth? Fate only knows, and before long, the race is on to see who will live forever and who is doomed to die.

"*Exceptional!!!*" Today's Books

ISBN 1-892339-10-2/$23 US

Join Sen. Chauncy, who longs to be virile enough to satisfy his young wife; an aging hippy named Rocky and his own wife, Laura, with disabling multiple sclerosis; a puzzling and disturbing old man whose motives are unknown; a young lifeguard with the hots for the senator's wife; an old woman and her cat, Lester; a vain former teen idol who craves a return to his glory days and the rest of the zany cast as they race to be the first to the Fountain of Youth in Glenn Meganck's fast, fun and furious adventure, IT'S A YOUNG, YOUNG WORLD, a story that explores the power and allure of youth in today's culture and the extreme effort some will exert to maintain or regain their own youthfulness in the face of growing old.

www.GLENNMEGANCK.COM

Also available from Beachfront

BUM RAP IN BRANSON

a Tony Kozol mystery

by J.R. Ripley

ISBN 1-892339-89-7/$25 US

"Taken separately, the elements that make up this seventh Tony Kozol novel might sound downright goofy. Country musician Kozol and his pal Rock Bottom are hired to play at "Kewpiecon," a Kewpie doll convention in Branson, Missouri. While there, they befriend--and defend--real-life country singer Jim Stafford, who stands accused of murdering rapper B.A.D. Spike. Spike, who was opening a controversial theater in Branson, has plenty of enemies--but Stafford is found standing over the body. When Kewpie merchandise is stolen and a conventioneer is murdered, new suspects emerge. From descriptions of the bizarre antics of the Kewpie conventioneers to the quirky characterization of Stafford (who older country fans will remember for his hit "Spiders and Snakes"), **Ripley spins a truly funny yarn that will have readers laughing out loud. An offbeat hit** that will appeal especially to country music fans." —Booklist

"**A delightfully funny mystery novel!**" Susan K. Scott
President-Bonniebrook Historical Society

"J. R. Ripley's Bum Rap In Branson is an exciting mystery
novel featuring Tony Kozol and Rock Bottom, who is drawn
into a bizarre recurrence of Kewpie dolls and murders, their
interconnection unknown. The latest entry in a genuinely
thrilling series, Bum Rap In Branson complicates Tony's
desire to just get by, have fun, and earn a few bucks playing
the guitar by saddling him with a murder accusation - he has
to clear his name fast to avoid singing in jail! **A viciously
delightful read for mystery/suspense enthusiasts!**"
—Midwest Book Review

"**Must read!**" — Today's Books, A Public News Service

CeeCee Kewpie has been placed in
the Witness Protection Program and
is believed to be living under an assumed
name in the American Southwest.

Also available from Beachfront

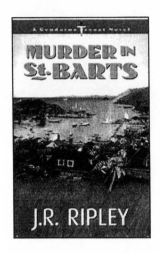

MURDER IN ST. BARTS

a Gendarme Charles Trenet novel

by J.R. Ripley

ISBN 1-892339-55-2/$25 US

An exciting new series by the critically acclaimed author of the Tony Kozol mysteries. Murder and romance fill the air on the exotic island of St. Barts in the French West Indies...

"It would be hard not to like Murder In St. Barts. The dialogue, the humor, and the sarcasm give us all something to enjoy." I Love A Mystery

"Trenet is a well-developed, likable character, and the novel offers an absorbing mystery set in the exotic playground of the rich and famous. An entertaining new series..." Booklist

"Exceptional!!!" Today's Books, a Public News Service

". . . A real treat." Library Journal

DISHING UP DEATH by Marie Celine

ISBN 1-892339-95-1/$25 U.S.

"Quirky and original with a real L.A. vibe. Great fun!"

J.R. Ripley

"...A rollicking tale meant to be fun to read—and it succeeds."
I Love A Mystery

Kitty prepares meals for the pampered pets of the rich and famous. Kitty lives in L.A. Where else? A graduate of a top culinary arts school, Kitty's passion for food and pets has led her to create her own business catering to the elite and demanding clientele of the City of Angels and Angles. Business is off to a slow but successful start when one of her clients' owners, fading rock star, Rich Evan, is found face down in one of Kitty's creations. Okay, it was the *Benny Had A Little Lamb*. Did we mention Rich was dead? Yep, deader than a canned mackerel. Seems the poor fellow has been poisoned. And Kitty is looking pretty good for the crime. With the assistance of her best friend, and an annoying L.A. County detective who can't make up his mind whether to arrest Kitty or marry her, Kitty must clear her name and save her business or her next job just may be working that long cafeteria line in the Big House.

"...An entertaining first mystery novel..."

Skokie Public Library

ISBN 1-892339-13-7/$25 US

The exciting and richly drawn follow up to the critically acclaimed novel MURDER IN ST. BARTS.

"An entertaining new series..." Booklist

Welcome to St. Barts, beautiful and sensual, vacation spot of models, moguls and movie stars and home to Gendarme Charles Trenet. Life is one sunny day after another and the life of the young gendarme is one of blissful tranquility—even his love life is looking up—that is, until the annual marbles tournament rolls around. The locals always look forward to the good-natured competition and this one looks to be the most exciting event yet. But what has made the stakes suddenly so high? And why does a seemingly friendly marbles competition seem to be at the center of an ugly plot that stirs the passions of all involved?

A seemingly harmless old man's murder raises questions that demand solutions and long kept island secrets and deceptions come to light as Gendarme Trenet doggedly tracks down the truth in this exciting sequel to Murder In St. Barts.

With Death Of A Cheat, Ripley brings us back to a world of rich characters and lush surroundings with a plot that digs in and never lets up till the last page is turned.

"The dialogue, the humor, and the sarcasm give us all something to enjoy."
I Love A Mystery

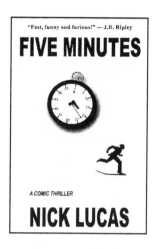

"Fast, funny and furious!" — J.R. Ripley

FIVE MINUTES

A COMIC THRILLER

NICK LUCAS

Five Minutes

a comic thriller by Nick Lucas

ISBN 1-892339-50-1 / $25 U.S.

"Debut novelist Lucas joins the growing list of Florida crime writers (Carl Hiaasen, Laurence Shames, Tim Dorsey) who mix capers with comedy. . .Readers will fall hard for this lovable loser as he struggles to stay alive while keeping his girlfriend from finding out what he is doing and his mom's pet pig from eating his stuff. Further adventures would be most welcome."

—Booklist

Nick Lucas' FIVE MINUTES starts at a brisk boil and never lets up until the last sentence is laid down in this gripping comic thriller about a man whose life has taken a quick and nasty turn for the worse. And goes downhill from there. . .

Look for upcoming Beachfront releases by featured authors including Marie Celine, Nick Lucas, Glenn Meganck, J.R. Ripley and more!

Beachfront Publishing
"Independent Books for Independent Minds."

BeachfrontEntertainment.com